REFLEX ACTION

"Freeze!" Fargo shouted to the three men standing over the girl.

"Son of a bitch," the thin-legged one rasped and his hand yanked at the gun on his hip. The others reached for their guns, bodies dipping as they drew. Fargo fired and the thin-legged one went up into the air as the shot slammed into his chest. Fargo fired again and the second man never straightened up to shoot, his body pitching facedown. The third had his revolver up and fired off two wild shots. Fargo fired again, and the dim orange firelight illuminated three still figures in a half-circle.

"Oh, God, oh, thank God," the girl breathed as Fargo leaned down, untied her wrist ropes and pulled her to her feet. She leaned against him, all softness with her high, round breasts pushing into his chest.

"This is getting to be a habit," Fargo muttered. . . .

CALICO
KILL

by

Jon Sharpe

A SIGNET BOOK

NEW AMERICAN LIBRARY

PUBLISHER'S NOTE

This book is a work of fiction. Names, characters, places, and incidents either are the product of the author's imagination or are used fictitiously, and any resemblance to actual persons, living or dead, events, or locales is entirely coincidental.

The first chapter of this book previously appeared in *Renegade Rebellion*, the seventy-first book in this series.

SIGNET TRADEMARK REG. U.S. PAT. OFF. AND FOREIGN COUNTRIES
REGISTERED TRADEMARK—MARCA REGISTRADA
HECHO EN CHICAGO, U.S.A.

SIGNET, SIGNET CLASSIC, MENTOR, ONYX, PLUME, MERIDIAN
AND NAL BOOKS are published by NAL PENGUIN INC.,
1633 Broadway, New York, New York 10019

First Printing, December, 1987

1 2 3 4 5 6 7 8 9

PRINTED IN THE UNITED STATES OF AMERICA

The Trailsman

Beginnings . . . they bend the tree and they mark the man. Skye Fargo was born when he was eighteen. Terror was his midwife, vengeance his first cry. Killing spawned Skye Fargo, ruthless, cold-blooded murder. Out of the acrid smoke of gunpowder still hanging in the air, he rose, cried out a promise never forgotten.

The Trailsman, they began to call him, all across the West: searcher, scout, hunter, the man who could see where others only looked, his skills for hire but not his soul, the man who lived each day to the fullest, yet trailed each tomorrow. Skye Fargo, the Trailsman, the seeker who could take the wildness of a land and the wanting of a woman and make them his own.

*1860, the Oklahoma Territory
just above the Kiamichi River, where
respectability and savagery hid behind
the same mask. . . .*

1

They were a lynching party. He'd seen enough of them to know at once. Only there was a difference. Not in type or attitude, those were usual enough. Six of them rode raw-faced and calloused, men who enjoyed lynching, taking coarse glee in their anticipation. Their victim rode in the center, and that was typical. Wrists tied behind the back. That was the same, too. But there the usual abruptly ended. No burly cowhand sat in tight-lipped defeat. No rangy horse thief rode with head bowed in guilty resignation. This victim was a slender figure in a dark-green blouse and skirt to match, high breasts bouncing in unison with her mount's stride, her medium-brown hair swept up and back from her forehead and held atop her head with a turtleshell clip.

Fargo moved through the thick stand of horse chestnut until he was almost parallel to the riders. He'd just wakened and breakfasted in the cool shade of the forest when he heard the horses nearing at a gallop. He had the Colt in hand as they appeared beyond the foliage along on open stretch of ground, and he had frowned at once. He never liked lynching parties, most self-serving and all aimed at shortcutting the law. Hanging was one thing, lynching another.

He'd swung onto the Ovaro and sent the magnificent black-and-white horse through the trees as he followed the riders, and now he reined to a halt as they came to a stop. The girl was young, with a pert, pugnacious face, a small upturned nose, and round cheeks, he took note. If she was afraid, she didn't show it. Anger and defiance held her face, and he saw medium-brown eyes flash at the men that surrounded her.

"This'll do," the front rider said, and indicated a buckeye with a long, low branch made for a lynch rope. He dismounted, a thin-faced man with thin lips, and reached up and pulled the girl from the saddle.

"Bastards," she snapped as she hit the ground.

"We ain't gonna let all that go to waste, are we, Hawks?" one of the others said out of thick lips and a puffy face.

"Meanin' what?" The man called Hawks frowned.

"We might as well enjoy her, first," the other one said. "The boss ain't gonna care any."

"Guess not," Hawks said, and the others left their saddles to gather around the girl. "Me first, though," Hawks agreed.

"Bastards," she hissed. "I didn't do it, damn you."

"You were seen, by more than enough folks," another man chimed in.

"Dooley saw you," the beefy-faced man said.

"He does nothing but lie and cheat in that card palace of his. He'd do the same anywhere," she snapped.

"Polly saw you," Hawks snarled.

"It wasn't me she saw," the girl shouted.

"And Cyril Dandridge saw you hightailing it down the road. Everybody knows that dark-red cape you wear," Hawks added.

"It was stolen a few days ago. I never knew it was missing," she said. She held to her story, Fargo observed. But then she'd have to do that much, he realized.

"Cut the damn talk and let's get a piece of her lyin' little ass," one of the others interrupted.

The thin-faced man closed his hand around the neck of the girl's blouse. "You better enjoy this, bitch, because it's going to be your last screw in this world." He laughed harshly.

"Go to hell," the girl flung back.

"Untie her wrists so's we can get her clothes off. I like my piece soft and naked when I get it," the man with the beefy face chortled.

"Just tear them off, dammit," another shouted impatiently.

Fargo's eyes swept the six men as they crowded around. His eyes took in the way each of them moved, the hang of their arms and the cut of their bodies, and he glanced at their hands and the six-guns on their gun belts.

"Wait," he heard the girl say, and returned his eyes to her. "I guess there's nothing else but to enjoy it if it's going to be my last time," she said.

"Count on it, tramp," Hawks growled.

"Then untie my hands and I'll make you enjoy it more," she said, and Fargo felt the frown press itself across his brow and he peered at the girl. She suddenly seemed resigned, an instant change in her that surprised him.

"Untie her," Hawks barked, and one of the others used a knife to slit the ropes holding her wrists. The girl brought her hands in front of her as she rubbed circulation back into her wrists. Slowly, she began to unbutton the blouse as Hawks waited in front of her, his eyes widening with anticipation. The others backed a few paces as they shifted their feet in coarse glee.

"This'll go quicker if you help," she said to Hawks, and the man stepped close to her and began to undo the lower buttons.

Fargo stared at the girl and felt the surprise still pushing at him when she suddenly exploded into action, her hand snapping out with the quickness of a young cat to close around the six-gun in the man's holster. She yanked it out in one lightning motion but she had to take precious split seconds to turn the gun in her hand and Hawks had the chance to fling himself away from her. But the shot caught him high on the shoulder and he let out a cry of pain as he fell back. Two of the nearest rushed at her as she whirled and brought the six-gun around to fire again. She got off another shot, which grazed the temple of the beefy-faced one.

"I'll take at least one of you with me, you rotten bastards," she screamed, fired again but with too much haste as the third man ducked, came in low, and tackled her around the knees. She went down as she fired a harmlessly wild shot before the others closed in on her. She fought with the fury of a wildcat cornered as they grabbed at her, and Fargo saw her legs kicking out, her hands trying to rake their faces with her nails. But they took hold of her, finally, Fargo saw as they yanked her to her feet. One of them smashed his hand across her face but drew only a curse from her.

"String her goddamn neck up," Hawks shouted, and Fargo saw him pressing a kerchief to his shoulder. "Just kill her."

The others obeyed and began to drag the girl to the tree, where one quickly looped the rope across the low, thick branch.

Fargo sent the Ovaro into a fast trot while he was still in the trees and emerged into the open less than a dozen yards from the man. He saw them hold on to the girl as they turned in surprise to stare at him.

"Party's over, gents," he said almost affably.

"Who the hell are you?" Hawks snapped.

"Delegate from the antilynching society," Fargo said. "Just let the girl go and we'll all stay friendly."

"The hell we will, mister. Get your ass out of here or we'll make it a double." Hawks pressed the kerchief harder against his shoulder.

"That so?" Fargo smiled, his hand resting on the butt of the big Colt at his hip. "I think I'll turn that down. So will the young lady. Now just let her go."

"She's a goddamn murdering bitch," one of the others shouted.

"The law call her that, yet?" Fargo inquired.

"We don't need to wait for the law. We know and lynchin's too good for her," Hawks snarled.

"They just want to lynch somebody," the girl snapped.

"She killed the finest man in town," one of the others said, a big, burly man with small eyes, avoiding the girl's accusation.

"We'll let the law decide that," Fargo said.

"I'll tell you one more time, mister. You ride fast or you're a dead man," Hawks rasped.

"Hang 'em both," one of the others put in.

"Can't ride off," Fargo said calmly.

"Why the hell not?" Hawks bit out.

"Against my principles. Got a prejudice against lynchings."

The one with the beefy face stared at the big man on the Ovaro. "You must be loco, mister. There are six of us," he said.

"Damn," Fargo swore. "My mama always told me to learn to count." He saw them exchange quick glances suddenly filled with uncertainty about this big, handsome man who faced them with unruffled calm. Fargo smiled inwardly. That would make their moves even more nervous and unsteady, and he surveyed the group again. Hawks was already no threat with his injured shoulder. The two men to his right, Fargo had already noted, were slow-moving and cumbersome. Their gun hands wouldn't be any faster. That left three standing alongside one another, two who might be of average quickness and the third, the burly figure, had thick-fingered, heavy hands more able to wield a smithy's tongs than a six-gun.

He waited and watched the uncertain glances harden. Like most men with more surface conceit that real courage, they had to prove themselves in front of each other and he expected that, too. As the two on his left started to draw their guns, he had the big Colt out of its holster and in his hand with one smooth, lightning-fast motion. The two shots sounded almost as one and the two men collapsed in a heap against each other, one with blood spreading from his chest, the other with his abdomen gushing.

Fargo swung the Colt as the two slow-moving figures at his right had just cleared their holsters.

14

He fired again and the two figures went down as though poleaxed. Fargo brought the Colt around and saw the thick-fingered man drop back, fear on his face as he kept his hand away from his holster. Hawks started to move for his gun, winced, and thought better of the idea.

"Drop your bun belts, nice and slow," Fargo said, and the two men carefully complied. "Get on your horse, honey," Fargo said to the girl, and watched her pull herself onto the mount with a flash of sturdy, well-turned calf. "Walk your horse next to me," he told her, and he turned as she came alongside. He began to walk the Ovaro very slowly, but his wild-creature hearing was tuned to the two figures he'd left standing behind him. He caught the faint sound the moment it came, and cursed inwardly, the soft slurred sound of leather suddenly creasing, the sliding hiss of a gun being pulled from its holster.

Fargo whirled in the saddle, the Colt steadied against his abdomen. It was the burly thick-fingered man, crouched on the ground with the gun just drawn out of the gun belt he'd dropped. The Trailsman fired as the man raised his six-gun, and the burly figure catapulted backward, straightened out in midair, and dropped flat onto its back. The man lay still except for a last gurgling sound that send tiny bubbles of red from his lips. "Damn fool," Fargo murmured, and his gaze bored into Hawk. The man pulled backward and slumped to one knee, only abject fear in his face.

"I won't try anything, honest, mister," he pleaded.

"Ride," Fargo said to the girl, and sent the Ovaro into a trot. He rode back into the horse chestnuts, following a deer path through the forest until he finally emerged onto a cleared slope where a stream bubbled its way downhill. He halted, swung to the ground, and watched the girl pull up and dismount. As the horses made for the stream he took her in more carefully and saw medium-brown eyes blink at him out of her pertly pretty face. But a tiny furrow touched her brow beneath the upswept hair and she regarded him with a mixture of gratefulness, curiosity, and a dollop of wariness.

"Why'd you do it?" she asked. "I'm grateful to you. Good God, I am. But why? You could've got yourself killed."

"Didn't expect that to happen." Fargo smiled and watched her regard him with her brown eyes narrowed.

"Guess not, seeing the way you handled that Colt," she said. "But why? You could've gone your way. Most would have."

Fargo shrugged. "Don't like lynch parties. Never have," he said.

"Then I'm grateful for that, too," she said. "Saying thank you doesn't sound near enough for having saved my neck, but I've no other words for it."

"They'll do," Fargo said. "You've a name?"

"Clover," she answered. "Clover Corrigan." Her eyes waited.

"Fargo . . . Skye Fargo. Some call me the Trailsman," he answered. "Now, you want to tell me your side of this, Clover Corrigan?"

She half-turned away for a moment and stared into space. She had a neat, solid figure, bustline very high and very round, a sturdy shape with curves in the right places but everything put together compactly. "I can't tell you much of anything," she said.

"Who was it they said you killed, the one they called the finest man in town?"

"Douglas Tremayne," she said.

"You knew him well?" Fargo asked, his eyes peering sharply at her.

"I worked for him," she said. "But I didn't kill him."

"Sounds like he was found dead and you were seen hightailing it," Fargo said.

"It wasn't me," she snapped angrily as he searched her face for the slightest sign of hesitation or slyness. But the only thing he saw flash in her pert face was anger and indignation.

"What about that dark-red cape they said you wore?" Fargo pressed.

"I didn't even know it was missing. Somebody took it to set me up."

"Why?"

"I don't know, dammit," she said, and Fargo saw the frown dig harder into her smooth brow as she stared back. "You don't believe me, do you?" she said accusingly, with a touch of hurt in her voice. She was either very clever or very innocent, he decided.

"I didn't say I didn't believe you," he answered.

"You as much as said it. Do you or don't you?" she insisted.

"Can't say," he answered honestly, and saw the instant anger flare in her brown eyes.

"Then you're the same as they were," she snapped.

"I'm not trying to lynch you," Fargo said quietly. She took in his answer with a glower. "You're asking me to just up and believe you. You've no right to ask that."

"Why not? I didn't do it."

"I've been fooled by words before. Pretty faces, too. Believing takes more."

"I haven't got more, not now," she said. "If I'd time, maybe I could find out more. I have to."

Fargo let his lips purse. She had an angry directness that held no guile in it. But, he reminded himself again, some women were mighty fine actresses. "You saying I should just let you go your way," he remarked.

"Yes, so's I can find the truth of it," she said.

"Or head for Texas," Fargo said, and she flared at once.

"You're making it awful hard to stay grateful," she threw at him.

"Let's ride and I'll listen some more. There's got to be more you can tell me, maybe more than you know there is," he said. She shrugged as the glower remained and climbed onto her horse with a quick, angry motion that made her high, round breasts bounce. Fargo began to lead a slow pace along the slope and kept his questions calmly casual. "I passed through Two Forks Corners a day ago. I take it this all happened back there," he said.

"Just outside of town, at Douglas Tremayne's house."

"Tell me about him."

"He was the town banker, leading citizen, popular with everybody. He was handsome, smooth, about forty but looked thirty."

"What'd Clover Corrigan do for him?" Fargo questioned.

"He hired me about a year ago. I helped him with whatever he needed, from making coffee, filling in as clerk at the bank, seeing to his appointments, to cleaning up his house. Sometimes he'd keep me late into the night writing down thoughts he had for a speech he was to make. Sometimes I'd fix dinner for him. I was part assistant, part maid."

"Anything else?" Fargo asked.

"No, nothing else," she snapped angrily. "I know that a lot of people thought that, but it wasn't true. Douglas Tremayne and I were never really close. For all the things he had me do for him, none of it was ever anything real important. I never did really know him. I always felt that."

Fargo watched the troubled frown wreathe her pertly pretty face. For all her anger and glower she had a lostness to her that reached out. She rode alongside him completely unaware that he had made a wide circle back toward Two Forks Corners. "Who were those men that wanted to string you up?" he asked.

"Hawks is a two-bit horse trader that Douglas Tremayne lent money when no one else would. Ahern, the big one, was the town smith and drunk. Douglas kept him in business, too, just as he did with the others. Hell, the whole town would've been with them by afternoon. Douglas Tremayne was everybody's friend. He sure wasn't the average banker," Clover said.

"Where'd they get to you?" Fargo asked.

"Came to my place. I'd just finished dressing when they dragged me out. I'd been home all night but they wouldn't believe it and I couldn't prove it," she said.

19

"Not with all the folks that saw you running," Fargo commented.

"Not me, dammit. They didn't see me," Clover exploded.

"You any ideas who they saw?" he asked, and watched her closely as she frowned in thought.

"No, not yet," she said slowly. "In that cape of mine, it could've been anybody, even a man."

"I suppose so," Fargo thought aloud. "Tremayne have a girlfriend?"

"I can't say for sure but I suspected he did. Once I found a blue slipper with a red bow in his closet, like someone forgot to pack it away before leaving in a hurry. As I said, for all I did for him, there was a lot about him I never got to know."

Fargo pulled up as they finished the full circle and let the Ovaro graze on a path of sweet clover. Two Forks Corners lay north, just beyond a thick stand of cottonwoods. All the time they'd talked, he'd watched her and had seen no sign of glibness or guile. But he saw her watching him, picking up the thoughts that moved across his mind.

"You've done a lot of asking and you're thinking all you've got is more words," she said.

"That's right." He smiled wryly.

"Because I can't give you more yet," she flared. "I've got to find out what happened myself."

"How do you figure to do that with a whole town waiting to lynch you?" Fargo questioned.

"I don't know." She frowned. "I'll find a way. There's got to be a way, someplace to start." She halted and turned a long glance at him. "You could help me."

"I already did that," he said.

"I know and that sort of makes me your responsibility," Clover tossed back with a smugness coming across her face.

"What?"

"Well, it does. Hawks is going to tell about you, and that Ovaro's easy to spot," she said. "They'll say I killed Douglas Tremayne and you helped me escape. You've got to help me."

"Damn, you've more than your share of brass," Fargo growled, and she shrugged and was suddenly quite happy with herself. But she did have hold of a kernel of fact and he didn't want more trouble. "I stopped a lynching. Nothing wrong in that," he said. "But I'll tell you what I'll do. I'm in these parts to break trail for a cattle drive down into Houston. I'm a week early. I'll help you, but we'll do it my way."

She smiled, a sudden explosion of sunniness that turned her pert prettiness into warm loveliness. "I'll settle for that," she said. Something, perhaps a fleeting expression in his lake-blue eyes, caught at her and she suddenly turned a suspicious glance at him. "What's your way?" she asked.

"First, I turn you over to the sheriff in Two Forks," he said.

"Hell, you will," she exploded. "Oh, no."

"For your own protection," Fargo said.

"So you can get off the hook by turning me in and going your way," she shouted. "Forget it. You're out for yourself, just like everybody else."

"Being grateful has a short life with you, doesn't it?" Fargo said.

"Yes, when it comes to being put in jail," she snapped.

Fargo glared at her. "Damn, you're a regular little cactus," he said. "But I'm into this and I'm going to help you in spite of your suspicious, short-tempered hide. I'm taking you in."

She sat alongside him and her eyes searched his face and he saw them suddenly soften. "Maybe I am too suspicious. Maybe I should be thankful to you," she said quietly, and then her voice tightened. "But I'm not," she hissed as she smashed both hands against him. He felt himself go sideways off the Ovaro at the unexpected force of the blow, tried to stop his fall, but his hand missed the saddle horn and he landed hard on the back of his neck. He felt the sharp pain as his head hit a rock and the world turned gray, then black, and he lay still in the sudden slumber of unconsciousness.

He hadn't any precise idea how long he lay'd lain there before he stirred, feeling the dull pain at the back of his head, and pulled his eyes open. He shook away fuzziness and the world took shape, the Ovaro first, standing nearby. Fargo pushed himself to his feet, his hand automatically going to the holster. "Damn," he swore as he found only empty leather, and he peered at the horse. She'd taken the big Sharps from the saddle holster, too, he saw and swore again under his breath. He pulled himself onto the Ovaro, let the last cobwebs clear from his mind, and saw the tracks where she'd turned and raced up the slope.

He started following the hoofprints and knew he wasn't at all certain whether he was following a scared, angry, brassy little package of fiery innocence or a very clever and determined pert-faced killer.

2

The trail was easy enough to pick up, Fargo quickly saw. Her horse had a corner missing on the right foreleg hoof that left a distinctive print. She'd taken a narrow trail up the slope at a gallop, hoof marks digging deep into the soft earth, and he followed at a trot and saw that she'd continued to ride fast and hard as the slope leveled off and the trail began to twist through a forest of ironwood. He followed, saw that she had slackened her pace only a little as the horse's strides shortened, then a hiss passed through his lips as he spotted the hoofprints that had suddenly swung in behind her. Unshod ponies, three of them. He swore silently as he followed. Indian pony tracks spread out before him, two sets moving to the sides and back into the trees, one continuing straight along the narrow trail.

Clover Corrigan's prints showed that she'd continued to push her horse, and Fargo slowed as the ground took a sharp rise. He reined to a sharp halt as he caught the sudden cry of pain from a dozen yards on, and he swung from the horse and moved forward on foot. The ironwoods thinned some at the end of the sudden rise, and as he crept forward, he saw the three Indians and the girl, all dismounted and one holding Clover Corrigan by the hair.

Fargo saw his Colt and the big Sharps lying on the ground and swore inwardly. She'd taken his guns and never got the chance to use them herself, which left him with only the throwing knife in its sheath around his calf. As he watched, one of the Indians, the tallest of the trio, gathered up the rifle and six-gun and swung onto his pony with the weapons. They were Wichita, Fargo saw as he glimpsed the tribal markings on a beaded belt the tall one wore around his waist. The Indian barked commands and the one holding Clover yanked her up by the hair and she uttered a yelp of pain. He wrapped a length of rawhide around the girl's waist and pulled her to his pony.

Fargo's hand crept down to his calf and he drew the double-edged, perfectly balanced throwing knife, known in some places as an Arkansas toothpick. But his lips pulled back in a grimace as he held the knife in his hand. Once he threw it, he'd have nothing left and he could take out only one with the throw, he pondered as he watched the third Indian mount his pony. They began to ride slowly off, the one pulling Clover along behind, and Fargo faded back to where he'd left the Ovaro, climbed onto the horse, and began to follow again. They had increased the pace a little, he saw as he caught up to them. Clover ran behind the one pony, breathing hard and holding on to the length of rawhide with both hands for balance.

Fargo stayed in the trees as he followed, moved another few yards closer, and waited for a better time or place to make a move. It was a risky game, he realized. They could have a hunting camp nearby with a half-dozen more braves, and he rode with his lips pressed into a thin line. The three braves stayed on the narrow trail and Fargo's eyes swept the trees ahead for a spot that might offer him a moment's advantage. But nothing helpful came into sight, and he realized he didn't dare wait any longer. He leaned from the saddle and picked up a length of broken branch, moving the Ovaro through the trees until he was almost parallel with the three horsemen. He saw Clover stumble, fall, and drag along the ground until she managed to pull herself to her feet again. The throwing knife in his belt, he raised the length of branch and tossed it into the trees on the other side of the three riders. It landed with a noisy, shrub-shaking sound, and the three Wichita instantly froze in place, their heads swiveling to peer into the trees on the other side.

Fargo drew the knife from his belt and dug heels into the side of the Ovaro. The horse responded with an instant thrust of its powerful hindquarter muscles. He was almost at a full gallop as he burst from the trees onto the narrow trail, the double-edged blade in his left hand. He sent it sweeping out in a slashing lunge at the closest of the three braves and the blade sliced across the back of the Indian's neck as he started to turn his head. Fargo saw the man's head fall sideways, a horizontal gusher of red erupting as he toppled from the saddle. The other two had swiveled on their ponies, drawing tomahawks at once, but Fargo had already yanked the pinto around and disappeared into the heavier tree cover. He reined up, leapt to the ground, and dropped to one knee as the two remaining Wichita slid from their ponies.

He saw the one holding the rawhide yank Clover

from her feet and pull her into the brush with him. The tall Indian crouched against a tree trunk with the rifle in his hands, held awkwardly, as a child holds a new and unfamiliar toy. Fargo waited silently as the Indian raised the rifle and began to move forward cautiously. The Wichita came toward him at a crouch, small eyes narrowed as he peered into the brush, and Fargo took a firmer grip on the handle of the throwing knife. He half-rose, gathered his powerful thigh muscles, and leapt into the air. The startled Wichita took precious split seconds to pull the trigger and Fargo had already dropped down into the brush when he fired a wild, hasty shot. But the thin double-edged blade was hurtling through the air, traveling the short distance almost with the speed of an arrow. Fargo heard the Indian's gargled cry and the soft, thudding sound as the blade struck. He lifted his head and saw the rifle fall from the man's hands, the blade buried to the hilt in the center of his chest. The Indian took a step back, sank to his knees, and pawed futilely at the still-quivering knife handle. Slowly, he fell backward and lay still.

Fargo had started to race forward to retrieve the rifle when the third Indian burst from the brush abandoning Clover as he ran to his pony. He leapt onto the animal's saddleless back with a diving bound. Fargo scooped the big Sharps from the ground and raised it to fire but held back as the Indian disappeared into the trees. He listened to the Wichita crashing his way in headlong flight and lowered the rifle.

Clover Corrigan came out of the brush, the length of rawhide still trailing from her waist. She stumbled toward him, fell against him, and he held her as she trembled for a moment, drawing in a deep breath that pressed the soft, high breasts into his chest. His hand on her back felt the sturdy strength of her compact body and she drew back after a moment to stare at him. Her medium-brown eyes somehow managed to hold gratefulness, contrition, and defiance.

"I'm glad you were able to pick up my trail," she murmured.

"That was the easy part," Fargo grunted.

"I never even heard them until they were on me," she said.

"You were too busy running. You're getting to be a pain in the ass."

Her lips thinned and she looked away. "I guess so," she said. She could switch from brassy stubborn defiance to lost little girl in the flick of an eyelid, he noted.

"I said I'd try to help you. You're not big on believing anyone, are you?" Fargo remarked.

"Same to you," she snapped at once. "You're not just believing me."

"One for you," he admitted.

"If you don't believe me, why do you want to help me?" Clover asked.

"Maybe to prove to myself I didn't make a mistake," Fargo said, and she didn't answer. "I'm still taking you in. It's best for you." She shrugged and blinked at him. "Your word on no more stunts?" he asked.

"No," she snapped.

"Damn, you're a hard-nose," Fargo said, and pulled the length of rawhide from her waist. "Then we'll use this." He wrapped the rawhide around her wrists with one quick, deft motion. "Let's go," he said, and helped her onto her horse. He climbed onto the Ovaro and led her mount alongside him by the cheekstrap. "The sheriff in Two Forks Corners, what's his name?" Fargo asked.

"Derrick," Clover said. "Sheriff Ed Derrick."

"How'd you come to work for Douglas Tremayne?" he asked.

"Left home when my pa died, started to go from town to town," she said. "Ran out of money when I reached Two Forks and needed a job."

"Why didn't you stay in any of the other towns?" Fargo questioned casually.

"Wrong bosses with wrong ideas." She speared him with a sharp, sidelong glance. "You don't just want to make small talk. Why the questions?" she asked.

"Trying to find out more about Clover Corrigan," he admitted.

"Wondering if I killed anybody else?" she snapped.

"Touchy, aren't you?" Fargo said.

"Being called a murderer always makes me touchy."

"Fill me in on some of those people who said they saw you run from Tremayne's house. Start with Dooley."

"He's a cardshark, runs a gambling place in town," Clover said. "He's a cheat and liar, too. Ed Dooley's no good."

"Polly?" Fargo queried.

"Polly runs the town whorehouse, only she has a piano player and calls it a dance hall," Clover answered.

"Cyril Dandridge?" Fargo asked.

"He supplies pots, pans, and houseware goods to traveling salesmen who ride the back country," Clover said. "Never liked the man. Oily, weasely creep. But Douglas Tremayne helped him with loans, helped all of them. I told you, he wasn't the usual banker."

"Seems not," Fargo agreed, and brought the horses out of the tree cover onto clear land. He went into a trot down the slope and held the pace until Two Forks Corners came into sight. His estimate of the town stayed the same as when he'd first passed through it a few days back. Like most towns that took on the trappings of respectability, the bank and the whorehouse, church and gambling den, sewing circle and saloon, all coexisted in a truce that recognized the realities of frontier life. He rode by the bank, red brick and impressive in a town of frame structures. The dance hall wore a weathered sign that proclaimed POLLY'S PEACHES in faded yellow letters.

Fargo steered the horses from the center of the street when he spied the two men standing outside a narrow building, one with a sheriff's star on his shirt, the other wearing a deputy's badge. The sheriff straightened up as he saw Clover, and his eyes went to the Ovaro and back to the big man astride the spectacular horse. Fargo returned the man's gaze, took in a stocky figure, a square face with shrewd eyes and a cynical twist to the mouth, the face of a man who wore authority but kept his own rules. The deputy was less stocky, with a young man's face that still wore honest openness.

"Never expected to see you, mister, after what I heard, much less with her," the sheriff said.

"Proof you shouldn't jump to conclusions," Fargo remarked.

"You did in five of our town's citizens, I was told," the sheriff said.

"I did in a lynch party. The young lady says she's innocent. They weren't listening," Fargo answered evenly. "I figured the best place for her would be locked up safe and protected until we get this straightened out."

"That's proper thinking, mister. I'm Sheriff Derrick. This is my deputy, Bill Bixby."

"Fargo . . . Skye Fargo," Skye said, and saw the young deputy's eyebrows lift.

"The Trailsman?" Bill Bixby asked, and Fargo nodded. "My pa was a good friend of Tom Hunter up Kansas way. He used to talk a lot about you."

Fargo gave him a slow smile. "Good man, Tom. Did a fair amount of trailbreaking for him."

"Now I understand what happened to Hawks and the others," the young deputy said with a trace of awe creeping into his voice. "Tom always said you were the very best with a trail, a gun, and a horse." Fargo half-shrugged and returned his gaze to the sheriff.

"I'll be leaving Clover Corrigan with you for now," he told him. "But I'll be stopping back, maybe tomorrow."

"Hah!" Clover spit out with cynical bitterness that he ignored.

"You did the right thing, Fargo," the sheriff said as Bixby helped Clover from her horse. The sheriff untied her wrist bonds and led her into the office and Fargo followed, watching as the man put Clover into one of two small, empty cells. The sheriff slammed the cell door shut and went outside, and Fargo met Clover's angry glower.

"You saved my neck twice, but right now I hate you," she bit out.

"I'm not riding out on you," Fargo said, and in her glower he saw the hope struggling to believe him. "Tremayne have an assistant at the bank?" he asked.

"Roger Weese," she said. "But he was never much more than a glorified clerk."

"I'll pay him a visit, anyway. Meanwhile, you stop fuming and start thinking."

"About what?" Clover asked.

"About everything you ever did for Tremayne, every little thing you ever saw or heard. Maybe you'll come up with something that'll help," Fargo said.

She was silent, and her glower followed him as he walked from the sheriff's office to where Derrick and young Bixby waited outside.

The sheriff regarded him with an almost amused glance. "You really figure you can help her?"

"Maybe," Fargo said. "If I decide she didn't do it."

"Damn few folks around here are going to buy that," Sheriff Derrick commented.

"That doesn't mean shit to me," Fargo said. "I just want the truth, whatever it is, and law, not lynching."

"Couldn't agree more," the sheriff said.

Fargo swung onto the Ovaro, nodded at the two men, and began to ride back through town as the first gray-purple of twilight began to filter down. He headed for the bank to follow through on the thought that had hung in his mind. Douglas Tremayne wouldn't be the first banker who had drawn the bitter hatred of someone whose home, farm, or business had been claimed. It was motive enough for killing, especially in this territory, where the law still came at the end of a six-gun. Fargo reined up in front of the bank and saw a thin, bespectacled figure starting to pull the door closed.

"Hold it a minute, friend," Fargo called, and the man paused and turned a thin, pinched face toward him.

"We're closing for the day," the man said.

"I just need a list," Fargo told him.

"A list?" the man echoed.

"A list of the foreclosure actions over the past few months and those still coming up," Fargo said.

The man's pinched face took on a frown. "Why?" he asked. "Who're you?"

"The usual reasons, looking for bargains I can pick up cheap. Name's Fargo," the Trailsman said blandly.

"I can't give you any such list," the man protested.

"According to law as I understand it, you have to give public notice of any and all foreclosure actions taken and pending," Fargo said, keeping his voice casual.

"I can't give you any such list because there is none," the man said. "Mr. Tremayne never foreclosed on anyone. He was a truly wonderful man." With an emphatic gesture, he pulled the door closed and disappeared inside.

Fargo spurred the Ovaro forward. Dusk had all but become dark and he rode with his lips a thin line. The visit to the bank had been a waste, a thought that foundered on Douglas Tremayne's unusual banking practices. The man had apparently been a very different kind of banker. Fargo frowned and reined to a halt again, this time in front of the gaming house. The quest for possible motives or leads was not unlike trout fishing, he reflected as he dismounted and went into the casino. If one spot didn't bring a nibble you looked for another.

The gaming house was only beginning to fill and he took in a dozen poker tables and two green-clothed dice tables and small bar against one wall. A half-dozen house players in shirt sleeves and green eyeshades were spread across the room, and a man in a flowered vest under a light gray frock coat watched the action from near the bar. He had a cardshark's eyes, Fargo decided, sharp and darting, taking everything in with quick glances. Curly black hair, a thin nose, and a pencil-thin mustache completed the man's face, and Fargo saw the quick-moving eyes take him in as he approached.

"Ed Dooley?" Fargo asked, and the man nodded. "Name's Fargo. Got a few questions about Clover Corrigan."

"You a friend of hers?" Ed Dooley asked.

"Sort of," Fargo said. "She says she's innocent."

"All I know is I saw her running."

"You see her close up?" Fargo questioned.

"Close enough. She cut into the bushes. She must've had a horse nearby," Dooley said. "I didn't think anything of it at the time. I figured she just didn't want to be seen leaving Tremayne's at that time of the morning. But I always figured she was his private pussy."

"Then you didn't see her up close," Fargo pressed.

"Hell, I saw that red cape of hers, no mistaking that. She did it. Leave it at that, mister."

"Soon as I'm sure," Fargo said. He slowly strolled from the gaming house and felt Ed Dooley's eyes following him. The exchange had proven only one thing: Dooley had seen a fleeing figure, nothing more. Maybe Clover. Maybe not. But for now, her claim to innocence still held up.

Outside, Fargo found a sharp night wind had blown up and he felt the tiredness come over him. He rode from town and up a hillside to where a gnarled honey locust grew beside a sandstone pillar. He set out his bedroll, undressed, and placed the Colt alongside his hand inside the bedroll. A deep sigh escaped him as he stretched out. He'd made a promise to a pert-faced wildcat, perhaps too much of one for the week's time he had. But more than that, had it been a promise to innocence or guilt, victim or Jezebel?

He closed his eyes and let sleep wipe away further wondering until the new day finally dawned and a bright sun quickly warmed the sandstone pillar. He found a trickle of a stream, washed, breakfasted on the sweet fruit of an elderberry bush, and slowly rode to town. He had decided to pay Clover a visit. Maybe the night had triggered some leads in her mind, he hoped. Sheriff Derrick and the young deputy stepped out of the sheriff's office as Fargo approached and both men halted as they saw him.

"You're real early," the sheriff said.

"Want a word with Clover," Fargo answered.

" 'Fraid you can't do that," the sheriff said, and Fargo felt the frown dig into his brow at once.

"Come again?" he asked.

"She's gone?" Sheriff Derrick said blandly.

"What in hell do you mean gone?" Fargo snapped.

"They took her," the sheriff said. "Man came with a warrant for her, signed by a district judge in McAlester."

"Dammit, I left her for you to keep here," Fargo said angrily.

"He had a warrant. Nothing I could do," Derrick said with a shrug. Fargo cast a glance at the deputy and saw Bixby's young face wearing an expression he could only describe as uncomfortable.

"You see this man?" Fargo questioned.

"Yes, sir. I saw him arrive. Had three others with him," Bixby said, and continued to look uncomfortable.

"You see the warrant?" Fargo pressed.

"No, sir. He only showed it to the sheriff," Bixby said, his eyes averted.

Fargo turned back to the sheriff, who waited with calm unconcern. "Where's the warrant?" Fargo barked.

"He took it back with him. I didn't think to have him leave it. My mistake," the sheriff said smoothly, and Fargo felt more than anger churning inside him. Something was wrong, the young deputy's discomfort only reinforcing the danger signals that had been set off inside him. Sheriff Derrick was playing it with smooth blandness and Fargo kept his anger inside himself.

"How long ago?" he asked.

"At least an hour. They're long gone by now," the sheriff said. "Sorry, but I couldn't ignore a warrant."

"Naturally not," Fargo said. "They take her horse with them?"

"Sure thing. They needed a horse for her," the sheriff said blandly, and Fargo slowly turned the Ovaro in a circle, his gaze dropping to the ground outside the sheriff's office. Plenty of traffic had passed by already. The ground was covered with hoofprints and wagon tracks. Fargo moved the Ovaro slowly along as he scanned the ground from one side of the street to the other.

"You're wasting your time," he heard Derrick say. "You'll never pick them up. They're long gone."

Fargo made no reply but his eyes narrowed as he kept scanning the ground, reading, unraveling, defining the way other men might try to decipher a puzzle. The confusion of prints covered the area, crossing and overlapping one another, but still he searched, his gaze riveted on the ground. A tiny sound of satisfaction came through his tightened lips as he finally saw what he had searched to pick out, hoofprints bunched together, horses moving together and overriding the other prints. He followed, staying with the prints even as wagon tracks all but obliterated them until he could pick up the marks again.

Four horses, he guessed, certain he'd found the trail he wanted even before he spied the print with the nicked right foreleg shoe. A grim smile touched his lips as the tracks grew clearer and swung away from town to head north into the high land. They stayed on the hill trails that led into rocky country, he saw, where only a sparse growth of buckeye and horse chestnut offered tree cover. They had continued on a twisting trail that wound between tall rock formations, limestone and granite mixed together, and Fargo estimated he'd traveled less than an hour when a house suddenly appeared, set between rock formations that stretched out on both sides of it.

Log-framed with a stone base, it was a large house, a wealthy man's house, with draped windows and a good slate roof. The tracks led right to the door, Fargo saw with a frown, and he moved the Ovaro up a narrow crevice in the rocks from where he could see the rear of the house. A small corral in the back held three riding horses and a buckboard, and a second fenced area was home to four white-faced cows and a handful of pigs that had appropriated one corner. Fargo brought the Ovaro out of the crevice and followed the hoofprints leading to the front door of the house.

The riders had halted outside with Clover, he saw, but they'd finally gone on again, the tracks moving off higher into the hills. But they had stopped, and he wanted to know why.

He swung to the ground when the door opened and a young woman stepped out. He found himself staring at a tall, willowy figure encased in a white, full-length housedress that outlined beautifully curved breasts and a long, narrow waist. A thin neck flowed upward to a face that was quite beautiful and made even more stunning by a streak of pure white hair, perhaps an inch wide, that ran the length of jet-black tresses. A thin nose, full, red lips, and eyes so deep and liquid that they seemed black completed the loveliness of her, and he guessed she was in her late twenties.

"Can I help you?" she asked in a low, throaty voice that almost purred.

"Maybe," Fargo said. "Some riders stopped here with a girl in tow. I'm looking for them."

"Who are you?" she asked.

"Name's Fargo, Skye Fargo," he said.

The liquid deep-brown eyes moved up and down the length of his powerful frame and halted on the chiseled handsomeness of his face. "You followed them here?" she asked.

"That's right." He nodded.

"You must be very good."

"Some folks call me the Trailsman," he said. "Why'd they stop here?"

Before the young woman could answer, the door burst open behind her and Fargo saw a man fill the doorway, a big man with a heavy face that still held strength and authority despite some sixty years on it, Fargo guessed. The man held on to the frame of the doorway with one big hand, gray hair cut short, his heavy face with a twitch in it, deep eyes holding an echo of pain in their harsh gaze. "What is it, Rosalyn?" the man asked as he peered at Fargo.

"Man followed them here. He wants to know why they stopped here with her," the young woman said, her eyes staying on Fargo.

"It was my brother who was killed," the man said, his voice booming, and Fargo saw the twitch in his face grow stronger. "I'm Abbot Tremayne," the man said, and his face suddenly reddened. "My brother, damn her soul," he thundered, and the red in his face deepened as he began to cough, a racking, harsh cough that shook his entire body.

"Please, Abbot, don't get yourself upset. You know you're not supposed to get upset," the young woman said, and turned to the man.

"Dammit, Rosalyn, I'll get as upset as I please," the man said, and another burst of coughing followed his words. His body shook again as the cough continued and his face grew an even deeper red. The young woman stepped to him and rested one hand on his arm.

"Please, Abbot, calm yourself. Look at what you're doing to yourself," she said soothingly in her low, purring voice. She had a voice that made everything she said sound sensuous, Fargo decided, and watched Abbot Tremayne drew a deep breath. The terrible coughing stopped and the redness began to drain from his face.

"I'm all right," he rasped. "I'm all right." He brought his gaze back to the big man who continued to wait quietly outside his door. "What're you waiting for, mister?"

"I didn't get my answer. Why'd they stop here with her?"

"To show me they had the murdering little bitch. I offered a reward for her," the man said. "I paid them and was glad to do it."

"And you don't care what they do with her?"

"Not one damn bit," Abbot Tremayne said, and his face began to redden again.

"She says she didn't do it."

"Of course she'd say that," the man boomed, and his voice broke on the edge of another cough. "What's it all to you, mister?"

"Made a promise to get at the truth of it," Fargo said.

"You've got the truth of it," Abbot Tremayne rasped, and broke into another seizure of the violent coughing.

The young woman went to him, took his arm, and began to turn him out of the doorway. "You go inside, Abbot. I'll take care of things here," she said. "You rest, dear, stay calm."

Abbot Tremayne disappeared into the house and the young woman stepped back outside. Her deep, liquid eyes surveyed the big man in front of her again. Though her appraisal was coolly thoughtful, sensuousness was a built-in part of her, Fargo decided.

"I'm Rosalyn Tremayne. My husband has been a sick man since he was stomped by a bull three years ago," she said. Fargo tried to halt the surprise from flooding his face, but Rosalyn Tremayne's small smile told him he hadn't succeeded. "I'm used to people being surprised," she said.

"I guess so," Fargo remarked.

"Abbot was a vigorous man despite his age five years ago. He ran the largest cattle ranch in these parts," Rosalyn Tremayne said. "He sold everything off since the accident."

"I can't stay to talk. Sorry," Fargo said, and turned to his horse.

"You're going after them, aren't you?"

"That's right."

"Why? You so sure she's innocent?" Rosalyn asked.

"No, but she deserves a fair chance and a fair trial," Fargo said. "I brought her in, and it seems that was a mistake. I aim to correct that much."

"You'll find them and take her back," Rosalyn said, regarding him with a long, appraising stare, the liquid brown eyes narrowed in thought.

"You can count on that."

A voice interrupted, booming out from inside the house. "Rosalyn, I need my morning brandy," Abbot Tremayne shouted.

"I'll be right there, dear," Rosalyn said, but she stepped to where Fargo had halted beside the Ovaro and her hand came out to close around his arm. "If I help you, will you help me?" she breathed, her voice a half-whisper, a tiny frown on her smooth brow.

"You want to spell that out more?" Fargo said carefully.

"I know where they're taking her. I'll tell you if you come back with her before you do anything else," Rosalyn Tremayne said.

"Why?" Fargo queried.

Rosalyn cast a quick glance back at the house. "I can't explain now. Just bring her back and I'll explain then," she said tersely. "Will you do it, Fargo?"

He let himself ponder for a moment and the answer was in the half-shrug he gave. "Talk fast," he growled.

"They're going to a line cabin up in the high hills. You'll be a long time following the trail they're on. Go straight up over that peak behind the house and down the other side. You'll come to a long line of junipers. Follow them and you'll reach the cabin. You might even get there when they do," the young woman said.

"Rosalyn, dammit," Abbot shouted from the house, and the woman stepped back. Her liquid eyes held on Fargo for another moment and then she turned and hurried into the house, her tall, graceful body moving smoothly, sensuously inside the long dress as she vanished into the house.

3

Fargo pulled himself onto the Ovaro and sent the horse on around the side of the big house, past the corral, and up into the rocky hillside. He chose a narrow passage that wound up between the rocks, and found the trail quickly grew steep. But the Ovaro's solid, powerful hindquarters drove him upward and the horse negotiated the narrow twists of the passage with surefooted skill. Wiry mountain brush poked out from the craggy rock, greenbrier and burdock with some mountain laurel, and he found the peak a long, hard climb. When he finally reached the top, he dismounted and let the pinto rest.

The slope down the other side held a half-dozen narrow passages, some hardly more than crevices between the rocks, and he chose the northernmost when he remounted and started downward. He let the Ovaro set his own pace and rode as far back in the saddle as he could to help counterbalance the steepness of the passage. The descent was difficult and slow and he saw the afternoon shadows lengthen over the hillsides. His thoughts idled as he rode, focusing first on Rosalyn Tremayne. She had been a surprise, her stunning beauty as unexpected as her cryptic bargain. But if Rosalyn Tremayne had spelled surprise, the sheriff had spelled trickery and betrayal. There'd been no warrant for Clover. She'd been turned over for a piece of the reward Abbot Tremayne had offered. The lying lawman would receive another visit, Fargo promised himself. But everything surrounding Clover Corrigan seemed to be taking on new dimensions, Fargo grimaced. He wanted to keep his promise to Clover and be on his way, and that meant fewer complications, not more. Though Rosalyn Tremayne's stunning sensuousness could be a welcome complication, he reflected, and put further thoughts aside as he spotted the line of junipers.

He swung into the trees where the land grew more level, put the pinto into a trot, and moved through the quickly darkening forest. He'd gone on for almost another hour when the last of the juniper forest came into view. He slowed and saw the land drop off suddenly just beyond the trees, and he spied the small cabin below, set in a rockbound hollow. Four horses were tethered off to one side. They hadn't been there long, their coats still glistened with a light patina of sweat.

Fargo brought the Ovaro to the edge of the junipers, swung from the horse, and took the big Sharps from its saddle holster. On foot, he moved down across the rocks, keeping to the shadows. Staying by the rocks, he sank down on one knee and surveyed the cabin again. The front door hung open; one window was cut into the wall facing him, and as he watched, one of the men came out with a bucket and went to a small well at the side of the house. Fargo watched silently as the man drew water and returned to the cabin.

Fargo's hand stayed motionless on the rifle. It would have been child's play to bring the man down, but the other two in the cabin would immediately make a hostage of Clover and that'd put an end to any advantage he might have. He had to find a way to get the three of them outside the cabin at once. He could hear muffled voices inside the cabin, but no screams from Clover and he was grateful for that much. Dark lowered itself over the hills and the bright glow of a fire came from inside the cabin. Another man emerged, this one tall and skinny-legged in worn Levi's, and went into the thick shrub on the other side of the cabin to reappear carrying an armful of small branches.

They left the cabin door open and a fitful stream of orange light reached out into the darkness of the night. Moving forward on steps as silent as a cougar's, Fargo made his way from the rocks to where he could see into the cabin through the open door. They had Clover on the floor against the far wall, and the thin-legged man sat close by her. The other two were sprawled on the floor in front of the fire, a half-dozen feet between them.

Fargo's eyes narrowed as he measured distances. He could certainly get two, probably a third, but he grimaced at the word. Probably wasn't good enough, not with Clover that close. He could hear their voices but little else, and he moved away from the direct line to the door. Staying crouched low, he hurried to the side of the cabin where he could hear without being seen. Their voices grew distinct as he settled on one knee almost against the outside wall of the cabin under the lone window. He heard Clover, anger and frustration in her tone.

"I told you. I don't know anything."

"You're being real dumb," one of the men said. "If you want to do it the hard way, we'll do it. We've got our orders and we've got all night."

"What are you doing?" Fargo heard Clover ask, sudden apprehension in her voice.

"Filling this bucket with hot coals," Fargo heard the man answer, and he carefully lifted his head to the window level to peer into the cabin. One of the three, a mustached figure with a harsh, still face, was shoveling still-glowing coals and ashes from the fireplace into a bucket. "We'll start with your feet, girlie. You'll talk by the time we reach your tits," he said.

"Bastards. Rotten, lousy bastards," Clover cursed.

"Get her shoes off," the man said, and Fargo saw the other two start to get to their feet.

Dropping low again, Fargo slipped away from beside the cabin, his mouth drawn tight as he surveyed the surroundings, and finally his gaze halted on the horses. They offered the only quick choice, and he hurried across the small hollow at a crouch, straightening only when he reached the four animals. He left Clover's tethered and undid the other three. He pulled them with him to face the cabin. With a hard slap on the rump, he sent one horse running forward and the other two followed. They'd go right past the open doorway, he knew, and he shrank back into the darkness, brought the rifle to his shoulder, and waited. He heard the shouts of consternation as the horses trotted past the doorway, and the thin-legged one was the first out, the other two running after him.

"Jesus, what the hell set them loose?" the man

called out as he started after the horses. "Didn't you tie them good?"

"I tied them, dammit," the harsh-faced one snapped.

Fargo stayed motionless until the three figures crossed paths in the dim glow from the doorway. He knew he could simply shoot them down, but the mercilessness of it never set right with him. He always liked to give a man a chance, even though he could almost predict what they'd do.

"Freeze," he called out, and the three figures skidded to a halt and turned toward the sound of his voice. They peered into the darkness and took a moment to find the dark bulk of his form. "Drop your guns," Fargo ordered.

"Son of a bitch," the thin-legged one swore, and Fargo saw his hand yank at the gun on his hip. The other two reached for their guns, bodies dipping as they started to draw. Fargo fired, and the thin-legged one almost flew into the air as the shot slammed into his chest. He spun and did a macabre little dance before collapsing onto the ground. Fargo fired again and the second figure never straightened up to shoot, his body pitching facedown. The third man got his revolver up and he fired off two shots, both too hasty and too wild. Fargo fired again and the dim orange stream of light illuminated three still figures lying almost in a half-circle.

Fargo rose and pushed the sour feeling away as he walked to the cabin. Clover's eyes were on the doorway as he entered, and he saw the flood of relief that engulfed her pert face.

"Oh, God, oh, thank God," she breathed.

Fargo strode to her, leaned down, untied her

wrist ropes, and pulled her to her feet. She leaned against him, all softness, the high, round breasts pushing into his chest.

"This is getting to be a habit," Fargo muttered. "One I'm going to break here and now."

"I know. You keep saving my neck," she said. "And I'm really grateful. But this time's different."

"How's that?" he inquired.

"Seeing as how my being here was your doing," she snapped briskly, and her eyes flared with anger.

He pursed his lips for a moment. "Damn, you're a brassbound package," he said. "But you've a point, this time. Taking you in was still the best thing for you. I didn't figure on a double-dealing sheriff."

"I'm not going back," she said.

"Let's get out of here and then we'll talk," Fargo answered, and led the way from the cabin. He saw Clover cast a glance at the three figures that carried nothing but grim satisfaction, and he waited as she got her horse. He moved up the steep and narrow passages, back the way he'd come across the mountain, and Clover stayed alongside him wherever possible.

"You know who sent those three?" he questioned.

"No," she said. "But I hope this satisfies you."

"About what?" He frowned.

"That I didn't do it," she returned.

"Why? Because they came after you? That doesn't prove a damn thing," Fargo said. "The lynch party wanted to hand out some necktie justice. These three were sure you know something. None of that proves you didn't do it."

She frowned back for a moment and let the frown slip into a glower. "Well, I didn't," she muttered.

"Didn't say you did, but you sure as hell haven't proved it yet," Fargo said, and steered the Ovaro up through a narrow passage that became almost pitch-black as the rocks rose on each side to shut out a weak moon.

"Where are we going?" Clover asked.

"Back to see Rosalyn Tremayne," Fargo said as the passage ended and he emerged onto a wider trail.

"Oh, no, we're not. Her husband offered a reward to see me dead," Clover bristled.

"And you'd be back there getting your skin blistered if it weren't for Rosalyn Tremayne," Fargo said, and drew a frown of surprise. "She told me where they were taking you and gave me the shortcut over the hills. I'd have been hours later reaching you otherwise."

"Why?" Clover asked. "Why would she help me?"

"Don't know, but her price for helping was that I come back with you," Fargo said.

Clover frowned into the night as she rode beside him. "It doesn't figure. I don't like it."

"I made a bargain. I'm keeping it," Fargo said, and moved the Ovaro into another narrow passage through the rockbound hills.

Clover fell behind him in silence, and when the passage widened, she came up alongside again but stayed quiet. He felt the tiredness sweeping over himself and the pinto as he pushed upward through the steep and dangerous passages, and when he found a rockbound alcove, the moon was past the midnight sky. He pulled into the area and dismounted.

"We'll bed down here and go on when it's day," he said, and Clover slid wearily from her horse. He set out his bedroll and tossed his poncho to her. "This is all rock. Wrap yourself in this," he said, and began to pull off clothes.

She took the poncho behind a tall boulder and he heard her shedding clothes. He was undressed, sitting up in his bedroll, when she came from behind the rock, wrapped inside the poncho and looking very small. She sank down beside the bedroll and her eyes lingered on the muscled beauty of his torso. "Why won't you just believe me?" she asked, and he marveled again at how she could switch from brassbound pugnaciousness to lost little girl with effortless ease.

"I've learned not to believe too much too soon," Fargo answered.

"There's such a thing as having faith in someone," she countered.

"Faith is for preachers," he grunted.

"I don't mean to push at you, but I guess I'd like somebody to believe me," she murmured.

"I'm trying. Leave it at that for now."

"I am real beholden to you for what you've done," she said. "I want you to know that. I know I get thorny, but I am grateful."

"You'd best get some sleep now," Fargo said, and saw Clover quickly lift one corner of the poncho when it slipped down to expose one round shoulder.

"Maybe it's good I'm so exhausted," she said.

"Why?" He frowned.

"Maybe I'd share that sleeping bag with you otherwise," Clover said, and lay down with only her head protruding from the poncho. She stayed wrapped inside it with a modesty that didn't fit her words, and he had to wonder what else about Clover Corrigan didn't match. He turned on his side and let sleep come at once. The rocky hills stayed silent except for the soft scurryings of white-footed deer mice.

The morning sun came and quickly baked the rocks, and he was awake and dressed before Clover sat up and rubbed sleep from her eyes. The poncho dropped down to reveal both sturdy, rounded shoulders and the soft curve of her high breasts before she grabbed it with both hands and pulled it up. She blinked up at him as he grinned.

"Bold by night, shy by day?" he asked.

"There are times for everything," she said, took the hand he offered, and pulled herself to her feet, still keeping a firm grip on the poncho.

"Get dressed. We've a good way to go," he said, and she scooped up her things and disappeared behind the rocks.

"I feel dusty," she called as she dressed. "There must be a pond someplace."

"Someplace," he said. "But first we get back to Rosalyn Tremayne."

Clover came from the rocks with the poncho folded neatly, and Fargo put it into his saddlebag and swung onto his horse. He set a faster pace through the narrow rockbound passages in the light of the day and he stopped only when he found a stand of white oaks burdened with sweet acorns, which furnished a wild breakfast.

The sun was in the noon sky when he began the descent on the other side of the mountain.

"What do you know about Rosalyn Tremayne?" he asked.

"I know everybody thinks she's especially beautiful," she sniffed.

"She is," Fargo said.

"She knows it, too," Clover muttered.

"What else do you know about her?"

"Not much. Saw her at the bank a few times and heard a few things," Clover said.

"Such as?"

"There was talk she got very unhappy with her husband. Seems she expected he'd turn the ranch over to her after he was hurt," Clover said.

"He didn't?" Fargo asked.

"He sold off his herd and land and give the money to some school for orphans," Clover said.

"Anything else?"

"No," Clover said, and continued on beside him in silence.

"You don't like her," Fargo said after a few moments. "Why?"

"I don't know why," Clover snapped in annoyance.

"Could be plain jealousy," Fargo commented.

"Go to hell," Clover murmured, and Fargo laughed as he led the way down hill.

The sun had slid into the deep of the afternoon when they reached Abbot Tremayne's house. He halted, peered down, and scanned the grounds with a searching survey. Satisfied that no one lurked outside, he led Clover behind a line of rocks. "You stay here," he told her. "And you damn well better be here when I get back."

"I'll be here. I want to find out what this is all about, too," she said. "Don't you go speaking for me."

"Wouldn't think of it," Fargo said, and walked the Ovaro down the rest of the passage to the house.

The door opened as he neared, and Rosalyn came out. He was reminded at once of how stunning she was as the sun glinted on the narrow, pure white streak through her onyx hair. A blue calico dress clothed her willowy figure and the deep, liquid eyes regarded him with faint surprise.

"You're alone," she remarked. "You didn't get her?"

"I got her," Fargo said evenly.

"Where is she?" Rosalyn Tremayne asked.

"Near enough," Fargo said.

Her lovely red lips formed a slow smile. "You're cautious. I like that," Rosalyn Tremayne murmured. "What about the others?"

"They made a fast trip," Fargo said, and drew a quizzical frown. "From stupid to dead," he finished.

Her lips pursed. "I'm not surprised."

"You know who they were."

"Cyril Dandridge's men," Rosalyn said. "They wanted the reward, I assume."

"More than the reward."

"I wouldn't know about that," Rosalyn answered.

"Why'd you want me to bring her back?" Fargo asked sharply.

"I want her to go away, get out of the territory. I don't want to see her go on trial," she said, and Fargo felt the frown dig into his brow. "I'll give her the money to disappear."

"Why?" Fargo asked.

"Abbot could never stand a trial. He'd die at all the dirty things that might come out," she said. "Douglas was always the apple of his eye, the kid brother, the favorite one. A trial could destroy everything he'd believed and cherished about Douglas for a lifetime."

"It might not harm his reputation."

"I can't take that chance. It would kill Abbot. I'd rather let her go free, help her get away, than risk my husband's life," Rosalyn Tremayne said.

"Clover Corrigan says she's innocent," Fargo ventured.

The young woman's lovely lips curled in a contempt-filled smile. "Rubbish. She was having a sordid little affair with Douglas. He was such an open, naïve person. I'm sure she seduced him into it," Rosalyn said. "And I'm sure he realized it wasn't right and tried to put an end to it. When he refused to bow to her threats, she shot him in a fit of rage and ran. Only enough people saw her."

"And you'd still help her get away."

"I told you, anything else would risk my husband's life. I really have no choice," Rosalyn said. "It's my way of repaying Abbot for all the things he did for me before the accident." She took a step closer to him and her hand came out to touch his arm. "Will you do it? Will you help me and ship her out of here? I've the money ready."

"I'll tell her. She'll make her own mind up on accepting."

"I'm giving her a chance to stay alive. She hangs on around here and they'll catch her, try her, and convict her, you can be sure of that," Rosalyn said.

She drew a little leather pouch from inside her dress. "Give this to her. It'll not only buy her stage ticket but give her enough to live on for a while. She'd be a fool not to take it and run."

"You might be right," Fargo admitted, and her hand dropped from his arm as he turned to the Ovaro. "I'll be in touch, tomorrow, I'd guess."

"Please. I want to talk to you about other things," Rosalyn said. "Things that could mean a lot to you."

"I always listen, especially to a beautiful woman."

"Good," she said and managed to give the single word a cover of sensuousness.

Fargo rode back into the hills and thought about the conversation. Rosalyn Tremayne had surprised him. She was capable of the unexpected. In more ways than one, he wagered silently. Her offer painted her as a model of deep faithful concern for her husband, yet she exuded waves of vibrant sensuousness. Maybe she was both, he pondered, a stunning woman too long denied. Perhaps he'd have the chance to find out. He smiled and turned off his thoughts as he reached the place where he'd left Clover. She rose to her feet as he came around the rocks, and her gaze held a mixture of concern, curiosity, and belligerence.

"She wants me to put you on the first stage for faraway places," Fargo said, and Clover stared back. He proceeded to tell her everything Rosalyn Tremayne had said, and when he finished, Clover glared at him.

"You tell her you'd do it?" she snapped.

"No," Fargo answered. "I told her I'd let you

make your own mind up on it. But I'd say maybe you ought to take her up on it."

"Why?" Clover frowned.

"Because she's right on some counts. You keep hanging around here and they'll catch you. If they do, you'll find it damn hard getting a fair trial from what I can tell unless you had the kind of proof nobody could look away from, and you don't have a damn thing, really," Fargo said.

"I'll get it. You said you'd help me," Clover cried.

"What if we don't come up with anything and they catch hold of you? Your goose is cooked then, honey," Fargo said. "This way you'd be far away and scot-free."

She stared into space for a moment and the pugnaciousness filled her pert face again as she returned her gaze to him. "No," she said firmly. "I won't be taking her offer. I won't run. That'd be as much as admitting I did it."

"It would, to some people. But you'd be saving your neck, and in time the truth might come out."

"I can't count on that. It'd always be hanging over me. No, I'm staying till I find the proof I need," she said, and her eyes took on a defiant boldness.

"Your decision," Fargo said, and silently gave her credit for sticking to her principles. It was the kind of stubbornness that added weight to her claims of innocence.

"You going to tell her?" Clover questioned with a sidelong glance.

"Tomorrow," Fargo said as he took in the shadows that blanketed the hills. "Let's ride while there's some daylight left. We've things to talk about."

"Find me some water first. I feel grimy," Clover said, and followed Fargo into the narrow paths that led to lower ground.

They had reached the low ground and night was descending fast when he spotted a whiptail lizard with a glistening hide, and he turned the Ovaro in the direction the reptile had come. He climbed a small hillock between some rocks and the pond lay in a scoop of stone on the other side. Clover almost leapt from her horse when she saw it.

"I'm not about to go hide so you can be modest," Fargo said as he dismounted.

"It'll be too dark for you to see in a few minutes. I can wait," she answered, and he laughed at the truth in her words. The small rock-lined hollow would be pitch-black until the moon had a chance to rise over the hills. He took his bedroll down and put it against one side of the rocks. "You said we'd things to talk about," Clover reminded him from the edge of the pond.

"Where are you going to stay? Maybe I'll come onto something. I'll need to talk to you," Fargo said.

"I've a friend, old Charlie Timkins. He's a recluse, you might say, lives alone in the woods outside town. He carves dolls and animals of wood and sells them at the general store in town. He'll let me stay with him."

"I'll go visit him with you tomorrow," Fargo said as the darkness descended. The rock hollow grew almost black and he heard Clover's footsteps move to the edge of the pond.

"Time to enjoy a bath," she said, a disembodied voice out of the dark, and he heard her pull off clothes and slide into the pond. Once in the water, she splashed noisily.

He undressed and strolled to the pond. He lowered himself in the water, which had already begun to cool, and heard Clover's voice, a sudden note of alarm in it.

"What are you doing?" she asked.

"Same thing you are. Didn't figure this was a private pond," he said. He stretched out and sent his body knifing through the water. He heard Clover move away and he dived, surfaced, let the water wash away the trail dust, and caught the sound of Clover as she left the pond. He stayed a spell longer until the water began to chill further and he saw the pale moonlight curl itself over the tall rocks to bathe the scoop of land in its silvery light.

He pulled himself from the pond and saw Clover wrapped in a large towel she'd obviously fetched from her saddlebag. It covered her completely. He moved to the Ovaro, rummaged through his own saddlebag, and came up with a hand towel he made do with to dry himself. Finished, he sank down on the bedroll and saw Clover turn to let her eyes move across the beauty of his muscled body.

"I don't want you to think the wrong thing," she said quietly.

"What would that be?"

"That it's so you'll believe me," she said.

"What are you talking about?" Fargo frowned.

"This," she said, and let the towel drop from around her.

She sat very straight and very naked in front of

him, breasts high and round, not large but beautifully firm and placed, and all smooth white with very light-pink nipples and light-pink areolae to match. Her body was compact, sturdy, with a short waist and broad shoulders, well-covered hips, and a slightly convex little belly with a modest triangle of tightly curled floss. She rose on firm, robust legs and came toward him, her body echoing the pert vivaciousness of her face.

She dropped to her knees in front of him and he felt himself responding at once to the sight of her vibrant, young body. Her arms slid around his neck and her mouth pressed hard against his and he felt the touch of her tongue at once, darting out, pulled back quickly and sent forward again. His hand closed around one high breast and found its soft firmness, the light-pink tip standing out, almost quivering, and he let his thumb go around the edge of it, tracing a simmering circle. Clover made a murmuring sound.

He gently pulled her down beside him, turned her onto her back, and caressed the high breasts. She quivered and her mouth opened wide, drawing him in hungrily. "Yes, oh, oh, mmmmmmmmm, yes," Clover breathed, and he felt her compact form move under his touch. He brought his lips down along her neck, nibbled his way lower, and closed gently around one firm white mound, pulling on the light-pink nipple, and Clover's convex little belly jiggled as she lifted her hips. "Oh, Oh . . . Jeez, aaaahmmmmm . . . mmmmmm . . . oh, yes, more, more," she murmured, arms tightening around his shoulders.

She twisted suddenly, a quick, demanding motion, and her sturdy young legs swiveled, her hips turned, and she was on top of him, pressing the tightly curled triangle across his thrusting organ, seeking, rubbing, crying out as she found his throbbing muscle with her lubricious lips.

"Aaaaah, ah, God," Clover cried out, and sank over him, pressing herself down all the way, and her rounded belly shook as she lifted and plunged down again, harder the second time and still harder the third. She continued to lift and plunge down, encompassing all of his pulsating shaft each time, falling into a rhythm that grew faster with each downward stroke. She fell forward and pressed her high, firm breasts into his face, seeking his lips first with one light-pink tip and then another. He let her set her own pace and she cried out with each plunge.

"Yes, oh, oh, oh so good, oh, Jeez," she murmured, and kept the soft funnel engulfing him. Clover pressed harder over him, her fingers dug into his chest, and suddenly her gasps turned into screams, short, urgent screams that began low and rose in pitch. "Yes, yes, yes," she cried out, and lifted her body, leaning back, and the high, round breasts shook. "Now. Oh, Jeez, now, now, now," Clover screamed, and tightened every part of her body against him, outside and inside, legs pressed into his hips, fingers dug into his chest, and inside, contractions that clutched at him, sweet pressures as her compact body pumped with frantic determination.

Her scream rose again, became a cry of sheer fulfillment, and she leaned back farther, throwing her head back, and small veins stood out at the base of her neck. She stiffened atop him until, almost with anger, she fell forward to lay over him, trembling, her breath coming in long, wheezing gasps. Finally she lay still but stayed on top of him, holding him inside her. "That was so good," she whispered into his chest.

"You explode, don't you?" he said. "You like taking charge."

"No, not always," she said, straightening her legs and sliding down to lie half across him. "But tonight I just had to hurry it that way. I couldn't stop myself."

"A long time between drinks?" Fargo smiled, and her face remained serious as she answered.

"A very long time. And never with someone like you. I guess it all came together inside me, gratefulness, wanting, and needing. You sorry?"

"Hell, no." Fargo laughed. "Maybe a little surprised."

"I meant what I said before. It wasn't so's you'll believe me. I do want that, though. It's important to me," Clover said.

"I'll keep trying. That's all I'll promise."

"Guess that'll have to do," she said, and a note of truculence came into her voice. She wriggled down and curled herself into the crook of his arm, the high, firm breasts lying partly across his chest. She sighed and her eyes took on a glint of smugness. "I'm not sleepy yet," she murmured, and he felt her fingers tracing a line down across his muscled abdomen. He smiled and brought his own hand up to cup it around one of the high breasts. "Aaaah," Clover murmured instantly as he caressed the light-pink nipple with his thumb. She turned, lifted herself at once, and brought her breasts up to his lips.

Her hands tightened against the back of his neck as he closed his mouth around one softly firm mound.

"Mmmmmm . . ." Clover breathed, and he felt himself rising, reaching up with a wave of excitement. He half-turned, pressed into Clover's rounded abdomen, and she gave a tiny gasp at the touch of him. "Oh, oh yes," she cried out, and moved her compact torso to rub against him. She sighed at the sensation of touch, her smooth belly against the hot pulsation of his maleness, and the sighs turned into soft, slurred breaths. Her hands came around to press into his buttocks and pull against him. "Please, oh, Jeez, Fargo . . . please," Clover gasped, and lifted her tight-curled nap and her sturdy thighs fell open. "Please, please, please." Tiny grunting noises followed each breathy cry.

He lifted and came forward, sliding into her dark moistness, and the gasps became a long cry of delight and she began to move with him at once. The terrible demanding haste of the first time replaced with a surging desire, she pushed and pulled back with his movements, matching his every thrust with her own, his every quickening with her urgency, and this time the young, sturdy legs tightened around his waist as she exploded with a gasping scream of vibrant ecstasy. Her high, round breasts jiggled as her entire body quivered with a succession of spasms. "Iiieee . . . aaaah, ah, ah, Jeez . . . Jeez," Clover half-screamed as she shook, quaked, and finally, with a sigh of terrible despair, sank back to lie still, legs still tight around him. "It's always over too quick," she murmured, and he lay half over her, his hand stroking her compact, vibrant body.

"You couldn't stand it if it lasted longer," he said, and she glowered at him.

"I'd like to try," she muttered, drawing in a deep sigh, and he lay beside her. She curled herself against him again and this time she closed her eyes. She was hard asleep in moments. Even in the depths of slumber, her face stayed pert and pugnacious, he saw, its own mixture of determined young woman and little girl. He half-turned and let sleep slide over him in the dark.

4

Clover shook her brown hair under the morning sun, swept it back from her forehead, and held it in place with a comb. "I'll need my clothes," she said. "We'll have to go to my place."

"Later," Fargo said. "I've some things to do first."

"Such as going back to tell Rosalyn Tremayne?" Clover said with just a trace of waspishness in her voice.

"That's one of them. You can breakfast on those black cherries just beyond the rocks."

"Hurry back. I don't like waiting."

"It'll be good for you, teach you self-discipline," Fargo said, and swung onto the pinto. He put the horse into a trot, rode downhill, and held the pace until he reached the bottom of the hills and made his way to Two Forks Corners. He felt the grim anger gathering inside him as he rode down Main Street, skirting a line of Conestogas taking on supplies at the general store.

The two figures standing outside the sheriff's office straightened up as they saw him approach, and he saw the sheriff take him in with a mixture of wariness and curiosity. The young deputy looked faintly uncomfortable as Fargo swung from the horse.

"Got a few things to say," Fargo growled. "In private."

"You keep an eye on things out here, Bixby," said the sheriff, and he followed Fargo into the office. The window curtain was more than halfway down, Fargo noted, and he turned to face the man, who continued to regard him warily.

Derrick walked to a wooden desk and half-sat, half-leaned his bulky frame against it. "Something bothering you, Fargo?"

"Got something for you," Fargo said.

"What's that?" Derrick asked.

"This," Fargo said as he swung, the blow traveling in a short arc but with all the power of his shoulder muscles behind it, a right hook that landed flush on the man's jaw. The sheriff spun, flying facedown across the desk to smash into the wooden chair on the other side. Fargo heard the chair splinter as the sheriff slammed into it and disappeared behind the desk. "It's a knuckle warrant," Fargo said. "Made especially for lying sheriffs."

He waited, rocking back on the heels of his feet, and watched Derrick pull himself up from behind the desk, a trickle of blood sliding down his jaw from one side of his mouth. The sheriff came around the desk and now his eyes were dark with rage.

"You bastard," Derrick breathed. "You're a dead man, but first I'm going to beat the shit out of you." He ended the vow with a bull-like charge, and Fargo came up onto his toes, stayed his ground, and measured distances. As Derrick reached him, Fargo stepped sideways and the man charged past him, tried to halt, but had too much momentum.

Fargo brought a smashing overhand right down on the back of the sheriff's neck as Derrick brushed by him and hit the floor on both knees.

But the lawman had a thick, bull-like neck and he pushed himself to his feet, whirled, and charged again, this time lashing out with a roundhouse left hook. Fargo blocked the blow and brought up a short, whistling uppercut that caught Derrick flush on the point of the jaw. The man's head snapped back and he staggered and fell with a twisting motion. He lay on the floor, his shoulders against the wooden desk, and blood came from both sides of his mouth now. Fargo took a long step to where the sheriff lay, reached down, and pulled him upright. Derrick's eyes opened, took a moment to focus and become small with hate.

"I want some answers out of you," Fargo said, and stepped back.

Derrick leaned back against the edge of the desk, and when he spoke, little sprays of blood came from his mouth. "I'll give you answers, you son of a bitch," Derrick spit out, and Fargo saw his hand fly to his holster, the draw quicker than Fargo expected. But Fargo's hand flew to the big Colt at his side and had the gun out and leveled as Derrick brought his six-gun up. Fargo fired, a single shot that slammed into the sheriff's chest, and the short-range force of the bullet sent Derrick catapulting onto the desk on his back. He lay there, legs dangling lifelessly, and Fargo pushed the Colt back into its holster as the young deputy burst into the office.

Fargo waited as Bill Bixby stared at the sheriff's body draped over the desk, and he met the deputy's eyes as they turned to him.

"He just resigned, the hard way," Fargo said calmly, and brushed past the younger man as he walked out of the room. He had one foot in the stirrup when he heard Bill Bixby call.

"Wait," the deputy said, and Fargo turned to see him hurry outside. "I've things to say."

"Say them quick," Fargo muttered.

"I'm sorry about the girl. I didn't have any part of him turning her over to them."

"She's all right. I got her," Fargo said, and watched the surprise flood Bixby's young face.

"He told me to mind my own business or I was fired, and I didn't want that. But it was wrong to look away. I should've let him fire me."

"Second sight's always easier than first. He was your boss," Fargo said understandingly. "I guess you're sheriff now."

"Guess so," the younger man said.

"Where'd he fit in with all this?" Fargo asked.

"They offered him a piece of the reward money for Clover Corrigan. I think that was it," Bixby said.

"Maybe it was for him but there's more."

"You believe Clover Corrigan? You think she didn't do it?" Bixby asked.

"I don't know, but something doesn't smell right. Either she's plain innocent or damn clever. I'm not sure and maybe some other folks aren't, either. I want to find out why."

Bill Bixby frowned into space for a moment. "Something doesn't smell right, I agree. I'm sheriff now, as you said, and if there's something wrong, I want to set it right," he said. "I don't want to be the kind of sheriff Derrick was. I was thinking maybe we could work together on this."

"Work together?" Fargo frowned.

"Behind the scenes. I'll nose around and see what I can come up with my way. You'll be doing the same your way and we'll get together on whatever we find out," Bixby said.

"I won't tell you where she is."

"I don't want to know that. As sheriff, I'd have to go bring her in. But I don't have to go trying to find her, not yet," Bixby said.

"True." Fargo nodded and studied Bill Bixby's face, peering hard at the younger man's waiting eyes. He saw nothing but openness in the ex-deputy's face. The man seemed honestly bothered by what had happened, and Fargo decided to take the offer at its face value. "I'll go along with you," he said.

"One thing more," Bill Bixby added, his young face grave. "We play the cards as they fall. If there's proof she didn't do it, I'll help you see that she goes free. If it turns out she did, you don't stop me from bringing her in."

"Fair enough," Fargo agreed.

"I'll be here if you want to reach me," Bixby said. "There's a room in the back with a cot and a stove."

"You'll be hearing from me," Fargo said, and climbed onto the Ovaro. He rode away at a fast trot and took a shortcut into the hills after he left town. Clover had seen him approach and rode out to meet him as he neared the spot where she'd waited.

"You took long enough," she grumbled.

"Town's got a new sheriff. Bill Bixby," Fargo remarked.

Clover studied him. "There's more than what you're saying," she decided.

"Derrick was a crook and a fool. Let's get your things," Fargo said, and started downhill as Clover decided against pressing further.

She took the lead when they began to draw near town, stayed in the trees, and reined up when they reached a road that branched off from the main one into town. He saw three houses, well down the narrow road, spaced with lots of land in between.

"I rented the smallest one from the Stallings. They live in the last house," Clover said.

Fargo edged a few dozen yards closer through the trees and drew to a halt. "You stay here. Might be somebody's watching your place."

"You'll find a big sack in the bedroom. Just toss all my blouses and skirts and Levi's into it. Same with the extra shoes," Clover said.

He pushed the pinto forward into the open and rode slowly to the house, his eyes sweeping the trees behind it and the heavy brush on both sides. He saw no signs of anyone near and he dismounted and went into the house. It consisted of only two rooms, one with a wood stove in one corner, the other boasting a wide, frame bed with brass fittings. He saw the sack on the floor and some of her clothes strewn about carelessly. He began to push clothes into the sack and halted before a closet built out from one wall of the room. He collected the rest of her things that hung there and lay on the floor of the closet, pushing everything into the sack until the small closet was empty. He started to turn away and paused as he saw a wrinkled bedsheet crumpled in one corner. He lifted it up and felt the frown dig hard into his brow as he found himself staring at the dark-red cape that lay under the sheet.

He continued to stare down at the red cape and it seemed to shimmer as he felt the churning inside him. Clover Corrigan's image whirled furiously through his mind. She could have fled, he heard himself thinking, taken Rosalyn Tremayne's offer, and been on her way to Texas. But she'd refused with high-sounding reasons and he'd begun to really believe her. In bed, she'd been more of the same, sweet, injured sincerity, and now the red cape seemed to fling itself up at him and he wondered if he'd been too hasty in believing. He dropped the sheet back over the cape and strode from the house with the sack of clothes while a kind of wary anger curled itself inside him.

He rode back into the trees where Clover waited, and her pert face brightened as he gave her the sack of clothes.

"Great," she said. "It'll be good to get into something different."

His eyes stayed on her as he chose his words carefully. "I decided not to include the red cape," he said casually, and saw the surprise flood her face as she snapped a glance at him. "That's right, the one you said had been stolen," he added. "I found it under the sheet in your closet."

Clover's eyes narrowed. "It was stolen," she said tightly.

"So you keep saying."

"Dammit, it was brought back, so it'd be found with my things. Whoever did it knew my place would be searched sooner or later. Hell, it was easy enough to do. I haven't been home for three days," Clover said.

Fargo turned the explanation in his mind. It held together, maybe too easily. But it couldn't be dismissed out of hand. "You're quick with answers, I'll give you that much," he said.

"Because they're true. When are you going to start believing in me?" Clover snapped angrily.

"When I can," he answered coldly, and saw her lips tighten.

"When will that be?" she muttered, and he marveled at how injured she managed to sound.

"No idea." Fargo shrugged.

"If you keep wondering about me, why do you keep helping me?" Clover asked.

"To satisfy myself, maybe," he answered.

"Feel free to back off," she snapped angrily at him, and put her horse into a canter.

He followed her through the forest terrain and made mental notes of trail marks he saw, a twisted limb, a stream, a double-trunked tree, a sudden stand of Indian pipes. It was an automatic thing with him, and he was at her heels when the log cabin came into sight.

Clover halted and jumped to the ground. The man that came from the cabin had a white, short beard and hair to match, crinkled blue eyes, and a limp. Clothed in old trousers, yellow suspenders over a gray undershirt, he embraced the girl with avuncular warmth.

"Clover Corrigan, I've been worrying about you. I was in town and heard all the talk," he said.

"I didn't do it."

"Hell, girl, I never believed you did," the man said, and Clover tossed Fargo a glance of satisfaction.

"I need a place to hide out," she told the man.

"Welcome," the man said, and looked at Fargo.

"This is Skye Fargo. He's been helping me," Clover said. "Charlie Timkins," she introduced.

"Glad to meet you, young feller," Charlie Timkins said. "Especially if you're helping Clover."

"Helping doesn't mean believing in Fargo's case," Clover said stiffly.

"Be glad for whatever it means," Fargo growled, and rode away without looking back.

The anger jabbed at him as he rode. If her injured indignation was an act, it was a good one, he grunted, and he sent the pinto into the low hills to the Tremayne house. When he came upon it, he saw Rosalyn Tremayne outside raking leaves away from the door, her tall, willowy figure in a black skirt with a white shirt hanging loose. He'd never seen anyone raking leaves in casual attire who could still look sensuous and sultry, he observed admiringly.

She came toward him at once and Fargo saw the top buttons of her shirt hung open to reveal the soft line of her breasts with provocative loveliness. He took Rosalyn Tremayne in again—the pure white streak through the onyx hair and the deep, liquid eyes—and decided that "stunning" was still the right word for her.

Her eyes questioned even as they moved across

his chiseled handsomeness with lingering appreciation. "You going to keep me waiting?" she asked with the echo of a smile touching her lips.

"She said no," Fargo answered.

"I half-expected as much," Rosalyn Tremayne said with the smile turning into bitterness. "That proves she did it."

"Some would say it proves the opposite," Fargo remarked. "Someone guilty would take the chance to run."

"It's not innocence that's keeping her here. It's unfinished business," Rosalyn snapped back. "Douglas had something she wants. She didn't have time to look for it after she killed him. That's what she's staying to find. I'm not the only one who thinks that."

"It seems that way," Fargo agreed as he thought about how Cyril Dandridge's men had been going to torture Clover to find out what she knew about something.

"But I didn't ask you back just to talk about her. I told you, there are other things. But first, come inside. Abbot wants to see you," Rosalyn said, and Fargo walked beside her into the house, enjoying the lovely line of one breast that revealed itself as her open-necked shirt moved. The house, he saw, was a sturdy structure, well-built and well-furnished with old prints of sporting scenes hanging on the walls of the living room.

Abbot Tremayne pulled himself out of a chair with effort as Fargo entered with Rosalyn, and he speared the Trailsman with a hard glare. "I'm doubling the reward for her," Tremayne said. "I figured you ought to know."

"Why?"

"I'm guessing you're the one that set her free," Tremayne said, his voice rising as his face reddened.

"How do you know she was set free?" Fargo questioned, and shot a glance at Rosalyn. Her even-featured face revealed nothing as she looked on impassively.

"I got supplies from town. Talk is that the three fellers that had her were found dead, with her gone. I figure it was you," the man said, and began to cough. Fargo made no reply and Abbot Tremayne's face grew more flushed. "You're making a mistake helping that little bitch. She killed the finest, most honorable man there ever was," he went on, and began to cough again, heavy, racking coughs this time.

"Don't, my dear. Don't get yourself excited," Rosalyn said soothingly, but her husband continued to cough.

"You set her free to do more killing, mister," the man accused. "You'll find out."

"I hope not."

"You bring her in and that reward's yours," Abbot Tremayne said. "Dammit, man, where's your conscience?" He began to cough again, deep, racking coughing that made his entire body shake, and Rosalyn went to him.

"Please, you shouldn't get so upset," she said as the man's face grew even more red and the coughing refused to stop.

Fargo watched as she led her husband from the room, the man moving with shuffling steps between fits of coughing. She closed the door behind her and

Fargo turned to examine the prints that hung from the walls until he heard her come back.

"I put him into bed," she said. "Excitement is bad for him and this whole thing has upset him terribly." She walked over to Fargo and halted only inches from him. "I need you, Fargo," she said.

"That's a good start." Fargo smiled.

"I want to hire you," she said.

"You just ruined a good start."

"Maybe not," Rosalyn Tremayne said. A tiny smile edged her lips, but the deep, liquid eyes stayed fathomless. "I want to get away from here. There's a place, way up in the Magazine Mountains."

"Arkansas," Fargo said, and she nodded.

"I've a map. There's everything from gold and silver to emeralds, topaz, opal, and other precious stones there. But I'll never be able to reach it without a really great guide," she said. "I'm going to go there, start a small mining operation."

"Why?" Fargo asked. "Seems to me you're well taken care of here with all the comfort you need."

"I'm not taken care of here. I'm a prisoner," Rosalyn Tremayne said with a flash of unexpected heat. "Abbot hasn't been a man since the accident. Three years is a long time time with no one to turn to, certainly no one around here. I've got to get away and start my own life again."

"What happens to your husband?" Fargo asked.

"I'll take him with me if he wants to come," she said. Her hand reached out to close around Fargo's arm, the liquid eyes swimming close in front of him. "I'll pay you well to get me there, Fargo, very well," Rosalyn Tremayne murmured in her low, purring voice.

"It's a real inviting offer. Sorry I can't take it," Fargo said.

The young woman's eyes stayed on him, grew wider. "Why not?" she asked, and sounded terribly surprised.

"I haven't the time."

"You've time to chase around helping a little murderess," Rosalyn Tremayne said, her tone sharpening instantly.

"Only a week, and she knows it. Your job would take a lot longer and I've a commitment to break trail for John Olsen up in Haldenville in a week from now," Fargo told her.

"I know Olsen. He used to buy steers from Abbot," Rosalyn said. "He can find someone else for a cattle drive, but I need the very best. I need you."

"It's too late for me to back out on him. Sorry."

Rosalyn took a step closer to him. "Think about it, please," she said, and her arms came up and slid around his neck and she closed her mouth over his. Her lips pressed softly and she had a musky odor to her that excited all of itself. The very tips of her breasts touched him tantalizingly. "That's to help you think about it," she murmured, and pulled back.

"It'll sure do that," Fargo remarked.

"There's more where that came from," Rosalyn said. "Do I surprise you?"

"Yes," he answered honestly. "On one hand you're the devoted, adoring wife who'd help a murderess go free to spare your husband more pain. On the other, you're more hungry than devoted."

"Seems a contradiction?" she said, a touch of rue in her half-smile.

"Seems that."

"Only it's not, if you can understand," Rosalyn said, and the deep, liquid eyes seemed to plead for understanding. "I'm grateful for all that Abbot did for me and I don't want him hurt. I'll do anything to prevent that. I'm also a woman who hasn't had a man for three years and someone such as you comes along. There's gratitude and loyalty and there's needing. Is that plain enough?"

"Plain enough," Fargo echoed.

"Come back and let's talk more about it, Fargo. Promise me that?" she asked.

"Why not?" Fargo said, and she walked to the door with him and watched as he climbed onto the pinto. She closed the door and he rode away, heading downhill unhurriedly. His answer had been no placating words. A woman such as Rosalyn Tremayne who talked of needing was definitely worth a return visit.

But now he wanted to pay young Bixby a visit and he sent the Ovaro toward Two Forks Corners as the night settled in. He wouldn't hold back, he had already decided. He'd made an honest pact with the new sheriff and he'd keep it. When he reached the town, he circled around to the back of the sheriff's office and saw the lamplight inside the building. He dismounted and knocked upon a narrow back door. Bixby opened it to admit him to a room that seemed hardly more than a large closet. Bixby motioned him to the lone, straight-backed chair while he sat down on the edge of a cot.

"Come up with anything?" Fargo questioned.

"Spoke to Cyril Dandridge, Ed Dooley, and Polly.

None of them did actually see Clover Corrigan. They saw a figure running in the red cape," Bixby said.

"Then it could've been anybody, even a man."

"Guess so," Bixby said. "But Douglas Tremayne had no enemies I know about. A broken love affair still seems the most likely motive for his being killed."

"Clover thinks he had a secret girlfriend. She once found a blue slipper with a red bow at his place," Fargo said.

"So she says," Bixby commented, and Fargo grimaced at the harsh truth in the answer. Grimly, he told the younger man of finding the red cape at Clover's house and her explanation.

"She could be right. There was time for anybody to put it back," Bixby conceded openly. "But then maybe she's just good with quick answers."

"I know," Fargo agreed. "Which puts us back where we started. No matter how things look, she could be innocent."

"Or guilty," Bixby said, and again Fargo had to concede the hard reality of his words.

"Who found Tremayne dead?" Fargo asked.

"Polly," Bixby said. "She said she was riding by and heard a shot and went to have a closer look. That's when she saw Clover Corrigan run from Tremayne's place. Dandridge saw her a ways farther down the road, and Ed Dooley after that."

"What time?" Fargo questioned.

Bill Bixby frowned in thought. "Must've been about four in the morning because it was nearly five when Polly woke up the sheriff."

"Doesn't it seem mighty strange that the town

madam, the local gambling operator, and a pots-and-pans supplier should all be that close to Tremayne's house at four o'clock in the morning?" Fargo ventured.

Bixby's frown deepened. "Yes, now that you put it that way."

"I'd say they were on their way to his place. But why at four o'clock in the morning? If they had business with him, why didn't they go see him at the bank?" Fargo ventured further, and Bill Bixby pursed his lips in thought.

"Beats me," the young sheriff said. "But I'm thinking I ought to ask some more questions."

"No," Fargo said. "You won't get straight answers and you'll put them on guard. Let me try my way. But first I think maybe we ought to know more about Douglas Tremayne."

"How you going to find that out?"

"Rosalyn Tremayne wants me to consider something for her. She might be willing to loosen her tongue some about her brother-in-law," Fargo said. "After that, I'll pay the town madam a visit."

"I'll keep nosing around. Might be I'll turn up something more," Bixby said, and Fargo nodded agreement as he left by the back door.

He rode from town and turned into the low hills, found a spot to bed down, and had just begun to unsaddle the horse when he noticed the pinto favoring its left foreleg. He lifted the leg at once and saw the shoe had come loose on one side, and his lips drew back in a grimace. There was a sudden new priority for the morning. Without a new shoe the horse would never be able to take ordinary riding, much less the rocky hill country. It meant a change of plans. He'd have to slowly make his way back to town and find the blacksmith who'd taken over for Ahern. If the man was busy, most of the morning could be used up. But he'd no choice, Fargo muttered to himself as he bedded down and realized there wasn't a lot of time left before he'd have to go on to his commitment. He closed his eyes, drew the night around himself, and slept soundly until the morning sun crept over the rocks to wake him.

He walked the horse downhill and climbed into the saddle only when he reached the flatland. As the Ovaro's limp worsened, he swung from the horse and walked the animal along the road that led to town. A good part of the morning was already gone, he saw by the sun, when he reached Two Forks Corners and found the new town smithy. There were four horses waiting ahead of him, he saw, and he swore silently as he left the Ovaro to be shod. He wouldn't let the morning go entirely to waste, Fargo decided as he walked down the street to the warehouse that carried the name CYRIL DANDRIDGE painted on one wall. *Household Supplies for the Traveling Salesmen* was stenciled under Dandridge's name, and Fargo pushed into the warehouse through a wide, swinging door.

Inside, he took in a large area with counters of pots, pans, iron skillets, and enameled coffeepots. Red baskets and brooms hung from the ceiling, and tin plates and wooden trenchers lined one wall. Stewpots, iron baking kettles, and fireplace grills took up another wall. He noted two side doors to the structure and brought his gaze to the man who emerged from a back room. Clover's description of

Cyril Dandridge had been on target, Fargo smiled inwardly. The man exuded an oily quality in the tight-skinned, weasellike cut of his features, in the quick, darting glances he threw out, but perhaps most of all in the unctuousness of his voice. " 'Morning, stranger. Come to set yourself up in business?" the man asked. "I'm Cyril Dandridge. You have the wagon, I've everything else you'll need."

"Not exactly." Fargo smiled genially. "Came by to ask about Clover Corrigan."

Cyril Dandridge's features tightened even more. "Who are you?" he asked, sharpness replacing the oil in his tone.

"Sort of a friend of hers."

"Don't come to me asking about her. All I know is she killed the finest banker a town ever had," Dandridge said.

"What'd you want to find out about her?" Fargo asked, keeping his voice bland.

"I didn't want to find anything out about her," Dandridge said.

"You sent your boys to bribe Derrick and make off with her."

Dandridge's tight face held its impassive mask. "That was all their idea. They wanted the reward money Abbot Tremayne offered," he said, and his eyes suddenly narrowed. "You're the one who went after her, aren't you?"

"Maybe," Fargo answered. "What did you want your boys to find out from her? What do you think she knows?"

"Nothing. I don't know what you're talking about, mister. Now, get out of here 'less you want to buy some pots and pans."

"Maybe some other time," Fargo said casually, and strolled from the warehouse. He walked unhurriedly to the blacksmith's shop, aware that Cyril Dandridge's eyes followed him until he was out of sight. The smith had just begun to fit a new shoe onto the Ovaro and Fargo leaned against the doorway of the shop as he waited. He smiled as he spotted Bill Bixby leading a drunk down the street and he watched the stream of wagons and riders that moved along the street. The sun was in the afternoon sky when the smith finished and Fargo cantered out of town and into the hills. He set a steady pace upward until he came to the rockbound clearing where Abbot Tremayne's house rested, and he saw Rosalyn hurry out as he rode to a halt and dismounted. She wore a deep-blue shirt and skirt and the liquid eyes surveyed him with surprise.

"I didn't expect you yet," she murmured.

"Need some questions answered now."

"Maybe it's just as well you've come now," Rosalyn said. "Abbot will want to talk to you. He's been very upset all day. I have, too, frankly. Come inside, please." She turned and Fargo followed her and enjoyed the sinuous movement of her waist and hips as she walked in front of him. Abbot Tremayne was in the living room and his head lifted as Fargo entered.

"You tell him, Rosalyn?" the man barked.

"No, I thought you'd want to," Rosalyn answered.

"She's been here, up in the rocks all morning, watching the house," Abbot Tremayne said.

"Who?" Fargo frowned.

"That damned little murderin' bitch, who else?"

Abbot Tremayne half-roared and a fit of coughing ended the outburst.

"Why would she be here?" Fargo queried.

"Waiting for a chance to kill me," the man snapped back. "My reward money is sending half the town out hunting for her. If she kills me, there won't be any reward. She's been moving up along the rocks. I got a quick look at her once."

"You see her?" Fargo asked Rosalyn.

"No," the young woman said. "But someone's been up there. I could feel someone watching the house and I heard a horse blowing air once."

Fargo felt his lips tighten. "You say you saw her. From in here?" he questioned.

"From that window," Abbot Tremayne said, and Fargo went to the window and peered out. The high rocks at one side of the house were visible but so were deep shadows and shafts of light from the fast-setting sun.

"Maybe you're imagining things," Fargo said.

"No, goddammit," the man barked, and a coughing fit seized him. "She kills us, it's on your damn conscience," he gasped and went into another paroxysm of coughing. Rosalyn went to him and made him sit back in a deep chair and the coughing finally lessened.

"I'll take a look around," Fargo said, and Rosalyn went outside with him.

"She'd be gone by now," Rosalyn said as he stopped at the Ovaro.

"I know. I just said that to calm him down," Fargo replied, and Rosalyn's eyes went to the high rocks that looked down at the house.

"She was here. I felt it," Rosalyn said.

"Forget that for now. I want you to tell me more about Douglas Tremayne."

Rosalyn cast a quick glance at the house. "I can't talk now, not with Abbot awake inside. He's very sharp, even with those terrible coughing spells, and he still has ears like a cat. Come back tonight, when he's asleep. We'll talk then," she said.

"All right, tonight," Fargo agreed, and climbed onto the pinto to ride off at a fast canter. He felt the grimness wrap itself around him as he headed downhill. Rosalyn and Tremayne were both on edge. They could well have simply had an attack of nerves, especially Tremayne. But he kept the Ovaro at a fast gait as dusk began to filter across the low hills and the rock formations took on strange and shadowy shapes. He reached the level land and the forest with enough light to pick out the marks and find his way to the log cabin before dusk turned to night.

Lamplight from inside the cabin sent a square streak of gold into the night from the open door and he halted alongside Clover's horse. He dismounted and ran his fingers across the horse's neck and withers. The fur still held dampness in it, the kind that clung to a horse that had been ridden hard and not sponged off. He frowned, brought his hands down from the horse, and stepped to the doorway. Clover looked up from a plate of corn fritters. Charlie Timkins sat in a corner painting the finishing details on a wooden figurine.

"Hello," Clover said. "Got anything to tell me?"

"Nothing important yet. Where've you been all day?"

"Out," she said, her face tightening almost imperceptibly.

"Out where?" Fargo asked.

"You going to start believing me?" she countered.

"Depends."

"That's not good enough. I'm tired of you doubting me," Clover said.

"That's a convenient answer," Fargo muttered.

"Convenient or not, that's it," Clover snapped.

"Your horse has had hard riding, galloping or high-hill country riding," Fargo said.

Clover's eyes narrowed. "Meaning what exactly?"

"You tell me." Fargo shrugged.

"I ran into six riders from town. They saw me and I had to go into hill country to lose them," Clover said, and Fargo nodded and kept his thoughts to himself. Once again Clover Corrigan had quick answers that could as easily be the truth as not. "Aren't you staying?" She frowned as he turned and walked into the night.

"Sorry. Got visits to make."

"I was waiting for you. I keep remembering the other night," she said.

He shook his head as he marveled at how instantly she could switch moods. As quickly as she came up with answers, he reflected. "Keep remembering," he said.

"Why can't you stay?" she glowered.

"You want to be cleared or be laid?" he asked harshly.

"Both," she said, lifting her chin.

"I'll do my best," he said, and rode away quickly. He sent the pinto through the thick forest with the increasing awareness that Clover Corrigan was becoming more and more of a pert-faced enigma. Believing in her was becoming both easier and harder, he decided as he sent the Ovaro out of the forest and into the hills.

When he reached the rockbound hollow in the low hill country, the Tremayne house was dark. He reined up outside, swung from the horse, and saw the front door open. Rosalyn slipped outside, her long, willowy body clad in a silver nightdress that reached the ground. A deep V neck let the curve of her breasts spill upward with exciting provocativeness. She motioned to him and he followed her into the house and down a narrow hallway to the far end. She pushed a door open and he found himself in a large room with a doublebed, the drapes pulled back on the windows to let the moonlight in.

"I've been sleeping here for years, now," she said. "Abbot has long, moaning dreams. He's in some world of his own when he sleeps. You can't wake him till morning." She lowered herself on the edge of the bed and her left breast all but spilled out of the neck of the nightdress, a long, lovely creamy mound. "Did you think about what I asked you?" Rosalyn said.

"Some," Fargo answered. "Can't see how I could go back on my word. They're depending on me."

"I think you ought to go visit John Olsen, talk to him. Maybe he could get someone else," Rosalyn said. "It'll be much more rewarding for you to go with me, Fargo, much more."

"I'll think about it some more," Fargo said, and lowered himself onto the edge of the bed beside her. Rosalyn's round, liquid eyes shimmered with a dark light.

"I know you will," she said, and her lips reached up to his and he felt the soft sweet pressure of her and once again, the exciting, faintly musky smell of her.

"I came to talk about Douglas Tremayne," he murmured between kisses.

"Later," Rosalyn breathed, and he felt her tongue come out, a quick, darting touch, and he opened his mouth and let his kiss grow hungrier. "Yes," she murmured, and her lips pressed back, opening, drawing him in. His hand found her shoulder, skin smooth and soft, and he slipped the strap of the nightdress down and watched the garment fall away to reveal lovely, creamy breasts, gracefully long, curving to rounded cups of fullness, each centered by an already firm, brown-pink nipple and a small brown-pink circle. His hand reached down and cupped one creamy mound, and he let his thumb move gently across the firm, brown-pink tip. Rosalyn's low, purring voice became a deep, silken sigh.

She lay fully back on the bed as he slid the nightdress from her, lifting her legs to help him pull the garment away, and he took in the long, thin waist, the flat belly with a tiny dark dot in the very center, flat hips, and a triangle of dense curliness as jet-black as her tresses. "Oh, oooooh," Rosalyn purred as he ran both hands down her body, caressing, pressing, his fingers lingering along all the curving places. He brought his face down and pressed his mouth over one creamy breast and Rosalyn's purr became a deep growl of pleasure. He pulled gently on the creamy mound, letting his tongue circle the brown-pink tip, and Rosalyn began to moan, a deep, purring moan that vibrated with enjoyment. Her hand came up, pushed her breast up deeper into his mouth, and the moan grew into dark, deep gasps of delight. She half-turned, pushed the other breast at him, and he took it, pulling on it. Rosalyn's fingers drew along the small of his back, digging in hard, almost raking him with her nails.

"Yes, ah, aaaaah, ah," she moaned, the sound deep inside her, and when his hands pushed through the dense, tightly curled triangle, the moan grew deeper, yet stronger. He pressed down and found a very round pubic mound rising to meet him. Rosalyn's long legs fell apart and she pushed her hips upward. He let his hand creep down into the soft folds of moist skin where her legs joined the dense triangle, drawing a fiery path down the insides of her thighs, and Rosalyn's moan became a deep, guttural cry. She pushed her hips upward further and held them lifted and shaking.

"Please, please, Fargo . . . oh, my God, please," she called to him. Her mouth opened and seemed to gulp in air. He brought his hand around to cup the warm, moist point of the triangle, and she half-screamed, the sound deep and vibrating, almost a growl, and her hand shot down to come against his and push. "Inside, inside, oh, God, inside, please," Rosalyn murmured.

He slowly pushed open the dark portal, felt the melting doors soft under his touch, and slid into the tender darkness. Rosalyn's scream came, deep and moaning and vibrating, as he played with her, caressing and stroking. She moaned and vibrated and gasped out half-words of pleasure, and her long legs lifted, sliding against his body in silent entreaty.

He brought his pulsating, anxious maleness to her and thrust inside her. She cried out, almost a gagging sound, and her hips began to tremble, quiver, and move up and down with long, sucking motions as he drew back and forth inside her. Her moans grew longer, drifting into one another until there was only a single, quivering sound, and her legs came up to lock behind the small of his back.

"Now, now," Rosalyn suddenly cried out, and the moaning grew deeper, more intense. "Now, now, now," she gasped again, and he felt her contractions grasp him, arms, legs, fingers, vagina, all of her tightening, contracting, quivering, and she engulfed him with her own sensuous delights. He felt her bringing herself to him, sweeping him along with her inner explosion and her deep, moaning cry became a growl flung into the darkness, animallike, and the onyx hair flew from side to side against the sheet, the white streak like a stroke of lightning against the night.

"Aaaaaagh . . . Jeeesus," Rosalyn cried out in a last gasping groan as she quivered and pumped against him, and he felt himself one with her, flesh capturing flesh, shared victory of the senses until she finally fell back with a groaning sigh. He moved to settle beside her and his eyes took in the long loveliness of her. He brushed the onyx hair back from where it fell across her face. Her eyes opened and the deep, liquid pools stared at him. "Reward enough, Fargo?" she murmured.

"Enough to make a man think real hard," he conceded. A tiny smile of satisfaction edged her lips, he saw. "For three years dry, there's no rust on you, I'll say that."

"A compliment?" Rosalyn laughed, a low, purring sound.

"Reckon so," Fargo said, and she leaned the long curve of her breasts into his chest. "I still want to talk about Douglas Tremayne," he said.

"I like a persistent man," Rosalyn said. "But I don't really know much about Douglas."

"He was your husband's kid brother." Fargo frowned.

"Yes, but I only knew him from a distance. He was only close with Abbot," Rosalyn said, her words almost an echo of what Clover had told him about Douglas Tremayne.

"Didn't you ever hear him talk to your husband about banking, problems, enemies?" Fargo questioned.

"No. Douglas didn't have any problems. I told you, he was a very private man. He shared things only with Abbot, who I think was more of a father than a brother to him," Rosalyn said. She stroked his chest with one hand. "I'm sorry I can't help you more," she said, and sounded honestly unhappy. He slowly rose from the bed and reached for his clothes.

"I'd best be going," he said.

"Come back? Tomorrow night?" she asked.

"No. I've other things to check out. The night after, maybe," Fargo said, and she rose and pressed her naked loveliness against him.

"She's taken you in, Fargo. She's clever, but

she's a murderess. Be careful," Rosalyn said. "I need you, remember."

"We'll talk some more," he promised, and she stayed in the room as he went down the hallway on the balls of his feet and slipped out the front door. He took the Ovaro down through the narrow hill passages, found a spot at the base of the hill country where a large box elder spread its thick branches, and bedded down for the night. He hadn't learned anything more about Douglas Tremayne, Fargo sighed contentedly, but the visit sure as hell hadn't been a waste of time. Before he dropped off to sleep, he set his plans for the next day in his mind and finally drew slumber around himself.

5

Fargo slept soundly, and when morning came, he found a pond, washed and dressed, and breakfasted on the fruits of a wild persimmon bush. He rode unhurriedly into Two Forks Corners and halted at the edge of town. He let the hours go by until he spotted Bill Bixby riding along the end of Main Street, and he moved into the clear where the young sheriff would see him. He turned at once and rode down the road as Bixby followed at a discreet distance, finally spurring his horse to catch up as Fargo halted beside a thin line of poplars.

"Good thinking," Bixby said. "I don't want folks to see us putting our heads together. You have anything new?"

"No, but I'm paying Dandridge's warehouse a visit tonight. There's got to be a reason why a pots-and-pans supplier was visiting the town banker at four o'clock in the morning."

Bixby nodded and sat back in the saddle. "Got a little something. Not worth much, I'm afraid," he said. "I questioned Weese at the bank about any unusual banking procedures Tremayne might have done. He said there weren't any. He told me that if anything else went on, Clover Corrigan would know. Also said he thought they were having an affair because sometimes Tremayne smelled of perfume when he came to work."

"Little things, but never ignore little things," Fargo mused aloud.

"We need more pieces to make a picture."

"I know. I keep getting mixed signals. Maybe after tonight," Fargo said, and stayed by the poplars as Bixby turned his horse and headed back to town. Tremayne had apparently been having an affair with somebody and all signs still pointed to Clover, Fargo pondered. But he refused to speculate further and started to take the pinto back into the hill country. When he neared Abbot Tremayne's house, he took a narrow passage that brought him up onto the rockbound terrain that looked down on the house. He moved the Ovaro slowly among the rocks and swore silently. If Clover had been there watching the house, the rock underfooting allowed no hoofprints to show. He dismounted behind a tall slab of sandstone and settled down to wait.

His eyes scanned the rocks and the small passages that cut back and forth through the land, but he saw nothing and heard nothing. The high rocky land was a quiet place. He could see the house below from where he waited, and any rider that came along the rocks one level down.

The day was at midafternoon when he saw Rosalyn emerge from the house pulling a sack of feed. She wore a gray shirt and skirt and the onyx tresses gleamed in the sunlight, the narrow, pure white streak even more pronounced. He watched her go to the corral behind the house and begin to mix the feed with water from a small trough for the pigs. With some surprise, he saw Abbot Tremayne come from the house and follow her to the corral. The man gestured angrily at her, obviously displeased over the way she'd mixed the feed. He was too far away to hear, but Fargo saw Rosalyn shout back and the dispute broke off when Tremayne went into a severe coughing spasm. The man all but doubled up, grabbing the corral fence for support while Rosalyn stood by. Finally, she took him by the arm and led him back into the house.

Fargo saw Abbot Tremayne pause in the doorway and look up at the rocks before finally shuffling into the house. The door slammed shut and Fargo stayed where he was as he waited, listened, and watched. But the rockbound hills stayed silent, and when the deep shadows of evening began to slide across the rocks, he stood up, swung onto the pinto, and started down the hills.

The night came quickly, long before he reached the bottom of the hill country, and when he rode into Two Forks Corners, most of the town was dark and still. He circled behind the buildings and dismounted when he reached Cyril Dandridge's warehouse. Slowly, he walked around the structure and decided that the back door seemed the least secure. He brought the double-edged throwing knife from its calf-holster and carefully worked the thin blade under the door latch, cutting into the wood until he heard the soft snap of the latch coming open.

He slipped inside the warehouse and carefully made his way around the place by a faint light from the windows. He saw only more of what he had seen during his daytime visit, and he found himself at the door to the back room from which Dandridge had emerged to greet him. He pressed the door and it didn't move and then he saw the padlock and felt the frown touch his brow. The padlock was a heavy one, he saw, and he cast a quick glance around and spied the small pile of empty burlap sacks. He gathered up most of the sacks, pressed them over the padlock, and pushed the barrel of the big Colt into the sacks. He fired and the sound was only a muffled popping noise, but when the burlap sacks dropped away, the padlock was shattered and open.

Fargo pressed the door open and went into a smaller room filled with cardboard cartons and wooden crates. He saw a hurricane lamp and turned it on low and the frown stayed on his brow as he surveyed the boxes. Pots, kettles, skillets, and pans were visible inside the crates; he opened some of the cartons to find only more of the same. He scanned the room again. There was no safe, no strongbox, no desk where cash might be hidden. The question hung in his mind: why was the room heavily padlocked if it carried only more of the things that were in the rest of the warehouse? He walked around the crates and cartons again. Most hadn't been opened yet and he chose a large crate first, ripped the top open, and began to remove the iron kettles and pots inside. He reached the bottom of the crate, stacking the contents on the floor beside him, but found only more of the same. He was about to turn aside when he stared at the bottom of the crate again, and the frown creased deeper into his brow. The slab of wood was raised perhaps nine inches from the very base of the crate. He tapped on it and heard the hollow thudding sound.

"It's a damn false bottom," he muttered aloud, and used his knife again to pry one corner up enough to get a grip on it with his hand. He strained and lifted, and the slab of flat wood came up. He heard the soft whistle escape his lips as he stared down at army-issue firearms, mostly revolvers with a few carbines included. He saw Remington-Beals army revolvers with trigger-guards, Remington-Rider pocket revolvers, five-shot double-action pieces, and rim-fire New Model Remington belt revolvers. Carefully, he put the false floor back into the crate and replaced all the kitchenware he'd taken out. He put the top strip back in place so it looked untouched, and proceeded to carefully pry open another of the cartons, saving the wire pieces that held it shut.

The carton held more kitchen equipment, which he removed until he reached the bottom: another false bottom, this one of cardboard, was raised almost a foot from the base. He lifted the cardboard section to peer down at a collection of government-issue coats, caps, and gloves.

"Damn," Fargo swore when he went through another crate and found new, unused army boots, footwear, socks, and pants all neatly and tightly packed together. His jaw throbbed with anger as he again carefully put everything back into place to the very last wire clip that held the carton together. Cyril Dandridge was doing a lot more than supplying pots and pans to traveling salesmen. He was running stolen government supplies and material for a fancy profit. But there was something more. He wasn't doing it alone. He had a silent partner, Douglas Tremayne. That's why he was paying a visit to the town's respected banker in the small hours of the morning.

"Damn," Fargo swore aloud again, and hurried from the warehouse.

Dandridge would find the signs of a break-in, come morning, but he wouldn't be certain of how much was actually discovered, Fargo murmured to himself as he climbed onto the pinto. Not that it made all that much difference now. There were other questions to answer.

He headed the horse for the stream of light that came from the dance hall. He wanted to find out how much of a masquerade Douglas Tremayne had carried on in his role of respectable banker. Hitching the horse outside, Fargo sauntered into the dance hall and peered through the thin haze of smoke. A half-dozen of Polly's peaches occupied a small, sawdust-covered dance floor with their shuffling partners. Three more girls in low-cut, tight-fitting party dresses leaned on the narrow bar next to a half-dozen men and eyed him with instant interest as he started across the floor. He halted when he saw a woman step in front of him, in her early thirties, he guessed, but far more attractive than the younger girls at the bar. He took in brown hair, a full figure in a tight red silk dress, and full breasts pushed out by the gathered neckline.

"Hello, handsome," she said. "You're new here."

"That's right." Fargo smiled and saw the woman's eyes go over him with an appreciative appraisal.

"What's your pleasure, big man?" she asked.

"Want to talk to Polly. I always start at the top."

"You're talking to her," the woman said.

Fargo felt a stab of surprise and realized he had expected an older woman with more paint, powder, and brassiness, a more typical madam for towns such as Two Forks Corners. "I want three things: strong bourbon, a hot woman, and some straight talk."

"I think we can supply all three of those." Polly smiled. "Come over here and sit, handsome," she said, and led the way to a corner table. As he sat down beside her, a figure appeared through a curtained doorway to halt a few feet away. Fargo took in the man, a towering brute of a figure, barefooted and bare-chested, wearing only a pair of loose trousers that didn't reach his ankles. The man stood at least six feet four, Fargo estimated. He had a flat-boned face, olive-skinned, that bore the marks of Indian blood mixed with something else, perhaps Mexican, framed by thick, straight black hair that came down to his shoulders.

"My personal bodyguard," the woman said. "He just stays close. He won't bother you, unless I tell him to," she added with a smile. She was a most attractive woman, Fargo decided, a most unusual madam. At a gesture from her, a waiter brought a shot glass of bourbon that Fargo tasted, rolling the liquid on his tongue, and smiled.

"So far so good," he said. His eyes moved across the girls on the floor. "I think you might have more trouble with the second one," he said. "I don't take to any of your peaches on the floor."

"I may have someone else in mind for you, big man. Let's get to the last. What'd you mean by straight talk?"

"About Clover Corrigan," Fargo said, downing the bourbon. "I'm told you found the feller she killed and saw her hightailing it."

"That's right," Polly said with a wariness coming into her tone. "What's it to you?"

"I want to bring her in and get the reward I hear is out for her. I figured you might be able to tell me something about her that might help me," Fargo said.

"Such as?"

"Where she lived. Where she came from. Whether she was the kind likely to hide or run. I'll settle for most anything you can tell me," Fargo said.

"I might be able to help you some. Give me another half-hour. Have some more bourbon. Then we can go upstairs. You can have that hot woman and the straight talk all rolled in one."

Fargo let his brows lift. "You?" he asked.

"Why not? I'll make an exception and take care of you myself. You look like you'd be worth it," Polly said.

"I'm right honored," Fargo said, and she ordered another bourbon for him as she made her way slowly across the room. He watched her as he sipped the drink. She took a roll of bills from the bartender and put them down inside the front of her dress, exchanged quick sallies with some of the customers, and murmured words to a few of the girls. Fargo eyed the towering figure to his left. The bodyguard hadn't so much as blinked and could have been carved of stone. It was a little over a half-hour when Polly made her way back to the table.

"Shall we go upstairs?" she said, making the question into a tantalizing invitation. Fargo rose to his feet and Polly murmured an aside to the near-naked giant as she passed; the man moved soundlessly through the curtained arch and disappeared.

Fargo followed her up the stairway to the first room on the second floor and noted that Polly's rear inside the tight dress revealed the beginnings of flabbiness. She led him into a large room with a large bed, frilled curtains on the windows, and deep pillows strewn around the floor. A heavy perfume hung in the air, and the moonlight filtered in through a lone window. The woman went to a white dresser covered with perfume and lotion bottles, took the money from inside her dress, and put it into a lock box in one of the drawers.

She turned to Fargo when she finished, a slow smile widening her lips. She unhooked clasps at the front of the dress, and the garment fell open. Large breasts spilled free, just the hint of sagging muscle in the way they hung loosely, yet still very attractive with large nipples on large dark-pink circles. She pushed the rest of the dress down and it slid to the ground. She wore nothing beneath it and stepped toward him with a body still firm, wide hips and legs that still held their shapeliness.

"We'll talk afterwards," she murmured. Fargo nodded agreement. It was perhaps better that way, he told himself. He wanted to question her and in the warm, lazy aftermath of sex she might be even more disposed to unguarded answers.

"Come on, big man," Polly murmured, and her hands began to unbutton his shirt. He slid his gun belt off and tossed it across a nearby chair as she took his shirt off and ran her hands across his powerfully muscled chest. He felt her hands hurrying to open his belt, reaching down into his trousers to undo buttons as he kicked off his boots. Her eyes had grown darkly turbulent and he heard the excitement in her quickened breaths. He felt himself rising, growing throbbingly firm for her as his trousers slid to the ground and he pulled off his drawers. Her hand came around his firmness, hot and smooth, and he heard her gasp out a short hard breath of air.

"Oh, Jesus, I knew you'd be special," she murmured. She fell back across the bed, still holding on to him, pulling him with her, and Polly's hand stroked his shaft with quick motions. Her wide hips lifted, her legs fell open, and she surprised him by the heat of her wanting. There was certainly no jaded playacting to her. She took her hand from around him only when he began to slide into her wide portal.

He had just let her wet warmth close around him and moved deeper into her when his ears caught the faint sound. He felt his body stiffen instantly and he started to pull out of her, but her legs came up to lock around his waist.

"Shit," Fargo muttered. He tried to roll with her, but she grabbed hold of the edge of the bed with her hands. He only had time to glimpse the naked torso of the towering figure before the club descended and he felt his head explode in sharp pain. Red and yellow lights burst inside him and he knew he was falling, floating in midair. A dark curtain dropped over him, shutting out the world, and a terrible pain flowed down through the back of his head, down his neck muscles, and he lay motionless, eyes closed, the gray curtain a shroud around him.

He tried to open his eyes but couldn't, and he lay still, no sensation in any part of his body. But, as if from a far distance, he heard Polly's voice. "He's out," he heard her say. "I think you smashed his head in." Her voice changed tone, seemed to come from even farther away. Perhaps they had thrown him from the bed, but he'd felt nothing. Yet somehow he could hear. A nerve end had been injured, probably in the base of his neck, perhaps in the spinal column, he thought almost abstractly. "He's the one that's been helping her," Fargo heard the woman say. "I knew it the minute he tried to sell me that story about the reward money. The fool took me for just one more empty-headed saloon girl he could ply for information."

Fargo felt himself cursing silently. She was right: he had underestimated the woman entirely and now he was paying for his mistake. He could think, his mind was clear enough, he realized, and the fact offered some slim thread of hope. But the rest of him stayed entirely without feeling. He tried to pull his eyelids open again and failed.

"Get him out of here. Dump him someplace outside town. I'll get rid of his clothes," he heard Polly say. Though he felt nothing at all, he knew he was being lifted and carried from the room. The giant was taking him someplace and Fargo cursed in silence and he felt nothing, saw nothing, the world a void that seemed not to exist. Time and movement were only measures of his mind now, awareness a thing of imagining. He was being carried away, probably on a horse now, maybe his horse, maybe not. He didn't even feel the night wind, and his thoughts continued to drift in their own spaceless void. He was nothingness and he wondered how much time had passed—moments, minutes, or hours? —and he cursed in silent helplessness. He lay surrounded by absolute emptiness and dimly he heard the sound of hoofbeats. His hearing still functioned, he realized with the relief of a drowning man catching at a branch. Suddenly, almost without realization at first, he felt sharp pain in the back of his neck, a sudden, stabbing burst of pain. Pain was feeling, he realized, and excitement spiraled inside him. Pain was welcome, wanted, a sign.

The pain came again, still as sharp, and now a throbbing accompanied it. Christ, he could feel something, Fargo swore silently, he could feel. The pain spread, moving up into the back of his head, and he almost laughed. He'd never thought there'd be a time when he'd so welcome pain. He pulled at his eyelids; they came open and he felt himself being jounced. He blinked, blinked again, and objects swam into focus. He saw the ground passing beneath his eyes, rocks and a piece of scrubby mountain growth. He was lying facedown across a saddle, bouncing on his stomach. The horse had a stiff jolting gait that bounced him with every step, and he was suddenly grateful for that. Somehow, the jolting had shaken away the paralysis of nerve and muscle and now he listened again and heard the sound of another horse. Very slowly, wincing with the pain, he turned his head just enough to peer forward and he saw the bare-torsoed shape of the giant bodyguard seated on a gray horse, leading the animal he was on behind. Fargo also saw long ears and a short mane. He was lying across a mule, he grunted, and the jolting gait suddenly explained itself.

He felt the night air sweep across his body and realized he was still stark-naked. He tried to move his arms and felt the ropes binding his wrists to-gether. Suddenly the giant brought his horse to a halt and Fargo dropped his head down at once. He kept his eyes closed as the man dismounted and walked back to the mule. With one hand, the giant pulled him from the back of the mule and dropped him onto the ground. Fargo stayed limp but real-ized his ankles were untied and he let the towering figure drag him across the ground by his wrists. He risked opening his eyes for a quick glance and saw rocks, a few scraggly pieces of brush, and a growth of tall Utah junipers. The man let him drop from his grip and Fargo saw they had halted at the edge of a cliff. He closed his eyes again as the huge figure turned to him, pulled a knife from the waist-band of the baggy trousers, and severed the wrist bonds. A naked man found at the bottom of a ravine would only bring curiosity and the shaking of heads. A naked man with his wrists bound could bring questions. Polly's instructions, Fargo was cer-tain. The giant wouldn't think that far ahead.

Fargo gathered the muscles of his calves as he let the giant pull him to the edge of the cliff. Ignoring the throbbing pain in his head, he waited a moment longer, let the man start to lift him from under the shoulders, and then he kicked out, a sudden, sharp motion that let him hook his ankle behind the man's calf. He pulled and the towering figure went down backward as one leg was yanked out from under him. Fargo rolled, and the man hit the ground only inches from him with the force of a falling tree. The giant figure turned, a frown on his broad, flat-boned face as he saw Fargo on his feet, and the frown held as much disbelief as surprise in it.

Fargo cast a glance at the ground and spotted a handful of loose rocks nearby. He darted to his left, scooped up a rock that barely fitted into his hand, and moved sideways as the giant started toward him. The man's thick, straight black hair swayed from one side to the other as he made little darting motions, and Fargo saw he held the knife in one hand. The giant feinted and Fargo stepped to his right, then went to his left as the man feinted again in the other direction. He moved sideways, glimpsed the edge of the cliff, and heard the sound of running water far below.

The giant suddenly made a grunting noise and lunged, and Fargo twisted away, bringing a looping right up with the rock clenched in his hand, but he was surprised by the huge man's quickness as he pulled back. The towering figure rushed forward again, this time sweeping out in a wide arc with the knife. Fargo ducked and felt the rush of air as the blade passed over his head. He drove a hard left into the man's abdomen, heard him grunt in pain, and followed with a straight right, the rock in his hand, into the same place. The huge figure staggered back with a gasp for air and Fargo caught the instant of pain that crossed the broad, flat face.

But the man came forward again, shaking off the blows that would have had ordinary men groveling on the ground. With a quickness that belied his size, the giant twisted and kicked out, and Fargo had time only to twist sideways enough to take the full force of the kick on his thigh. He felt pain shoot up his leg and he fell sideways, managing to stay on one knee, and saw the man rushing at him. He threw himself to the right as the knifeblade whistled past his ear; he rolled and almost cried out at the pain that shot along his neck. The rock fell from his hand and he looked back to see the towering figure charging, the knife raised to plunge down into him. He rolled again, cursed at the pain, and managed to scoop the rock up as he regained his feet and half-ran, half-fell into the thick brush beneath the Utah junipers.

He halted, turned, and saw the man pause at the edge of the brush, peering into the darker area with his eyes like little black gimlets. Fargo braced himself and shook a piece of brush with his left hand, and the giant let out a roar of triumph as he charged. Fargo half-rose and flung the rock with all the strength of his muscled shoulder and upper arm. The stone smashed into the man's broad face with crashing force and Fargo watched the giant figure stop, stagger backward, and drop to one knee at the edge of the brush. Bleeding from cheekbones, nose, and mouth, the man stayed on one knee and shook his head as a bull shakes itself before attempting to charge again. Fargo took three long strides forward and lifted a whistling right that caught the man on the point of the jaw. The giant figure's head snapped back and the man fell onto his back.

Fargo stepped in to scoop up the knife he saw fall from the man's hand; he had begun to bend down to reach the blade when a huge leg kicked out and Fargo groaned in pain as the blow caught him in the belly. He felt himself thrown backward by the force of the kick, and the wiry underbrush scraped his naked body when he landed in it. He fought for breath, pulled himself halfway up in front of one of the gray-barked junipers, and saw that the giant figure had seized the knife again. The man came at him, his face a mask of dripping blood, thick, straight black hair shaking as he began to run. He held the knife up, ready to strike down or sideways with it, and Fargo fought again for breath. The towering figure gathered speed and charged like a wild buffalo. Holding off till the last moment and then rolling aside was impossible, Fargo realized. The thick brush would cling and slow him down just enough to let the knife slice him in two. He glanced back, grimaced, and moved to his right as he backed a few steps closer to the juniper. He reached the right spot as the raging, bloodied shape charged, only inches from him now. The man roared as he raised the knife high to plunge it into the crouching foe in front of him and Fargo dived, but not sideways. He flung himself low and forward, his body slamming into the man at the ankles, and he felt the giant figure catapult forward over him. He twisted as he hit the ground to see the man's bloodied face slam full-force into the craggy bark of the tree.

The giant figure clung to the tree for a moment and then slowly began to slide to the ground. Fargo leapt up, whirled, and drove a kick into the man's naked back with all the force of his own powerful leg muscles. He heard the sound of the small spinal bones snapping, and the huge figure stopped sliding down. The knife dropped from his hand and he lay motionless, face against the base of the tree, not unlike some strange forest growth.

Fargo stepped from the brush, sank down for a minute, and drew in deep gulps of air. His neck still throbbed, his leg hurt, and his belly still quivered as he drew in breath. But he was alive—naked as the day he was born, but alive. Slowly, he stood up, rested a few minutes more against a rock, and made his way to the horse and pulled himself into the saddle. He rode slowly down through low hill country in the dark, the mule following, and by the time he neared Two Forks Corners the pain that racked his body had begun to subside. But the anger gathered inside him as he entered the still-dark town and made his way to the rear of the dark dance hall.

He still wanted the answers he had originally come to get. He had made a mistake, underestimated Polly's sharp intelligence. Now she was going to learn about underestimating.

6

A narrow wooden stairway alongside the rear of the dance hall rose to the second floor, Fargo saw. He slid his naked body from the horse and began to climb the steps, testing each one before he stepped on it. When he reached the top, he closed his hand around the knob of the door and turned, and the door opened at once. He slipped into a corridor— rooms with the doors closed on both sides—and he crept down toward the last closed door near the inside stairway. He leaned his face against the door and smelled the perfume-laden air from inside. He slowly turned the knob, dropping low onto his haunches as the door opened.

He heard the sound of her even breathing and saw her shape in the large bed as he straightened and stepped into the room. He closed the door as silently as he'd opened it, and as he crossed to the bed, he saw his clothes were still in a pile on the floor. He halted at the side of the bed. Polly slept in a very plain nightgown, he saw, and in the half-light looked even younger than she was. With one quick, lithe motion he swung himself over her to rest with his torso pressing down onto her little pubic mound. He saw her eyes snap open and stare at him for a moment as she came awake.

"We were interrupted," he said softly.

The woman's lips parted and she started to form a scream, but Fargo's hand shot out and closed around her throat. "Don't even think about it or I'll break your clever little neck," he growled, and saw her pull her mouth closed. "You want to take up where we left off or do we go right to that straight talk you were going to give me?" he asked.

"Go to hell," the woman hissed.

Fargo's hand came around in a smashing slap that drove her face into the pillow and she yelped in pain. "Now, you all but had me killed and left naked at the bottom of a ravine," Fargo said as her eyes came back to him. "I still ache and hurt all over and I'm not in the mood for playing any more games. Now, you talk or by God this place is going to need a new madam." For emphasis, his hand closed around her neck again with more pressure, and as his fingers tightened, her face drained of color.

"All right, damn you," Polly breathed, a hoarse sound, and he relaxed his grip.

"You found Tremayne because you were there to visit with him. Why at that hour of the morning?" Fargo shot at her.

"To give him his cut of the week's take."

"Go on," Fargo said, and realized he wasn't surprised.

"When he took over the bank he told me he'd enough money and influence to close me up, buy the house and land, and send me packing. He did, I realized, and when he offered his deal, I took it," Polly said. "He got twenty-five percent of the take each week."

"He was a silent partner," Fargo muttered, and she nodded.

"He wanted more fast money than the banking business could give him, money he could stash away for himself," she said.

"He did the same with Dandridge, didn't he?" Fargo asked. "Became a silent partner in Dandridge's stolen-goods operation."

"Yes." She nodded again. "Only he financed Dandridge's whole operation for his share."

"He had twenty-five percent of Ed Dooley's gambling-house take, too," Fargo said, and Polly nodded once more.

"He knew Dooley was wanted in Kansas under another name and threatened to turn him in if he didn't get a piece of the action," Polly said.

"How come you all stood still for it?" Fargo asked.

"He told us it was all down somewhere in black and white and it'd be found if anything happened to him," she said. "Nobody wanted to take that chance. We decided we could all live with it."

"Maybe one of you killed him. Maybe one of you decided not to go on any longer," Fargo put out.

The woman made a face of disgust. "Never. We got used to it, and he saw to it that if we needed extra money we got it," she said. "It was an arrangement and it worked. Nobody would risk blowing it up and having the truth come out. She killed him, for her own damn good reasons."

"Such as?" Fargo frowned.

"Douglas Tremayne stashed away one hell of a lot of money over the years. She probably learned about it and wanted a piece of it. When he said no, she killed him, probably in a fight, because she didn't get what she wanted."

"Which was?"

"Where he has the money hidden," the woman said. "That's why she's staying around. She figures to find a way to get back into his place and find where he's put all that money. She worked with him long enough. She's got a good chance at finding it."

"So what? It's money you've all written off. Why this hurry to get her lynched or bushwhacked?" Fargo questioned.

"We can't afford to have her on trial before a district judge. It'd all come out and we'd all be in a cell. If she finds where he hid the money, she might also find whatever he put down in black and white. We can't take that chance, either," Polly said. "It'd all have been done and over if you hadn't decided to help the little bitch."

Fargo swung from atop her, landing lightly on the balls of his feet, and began to pull on his clothes. "You damn near had me killed. I ought to break your neck for that. I'm going to think some more about it, and about what you've just told me."

"I'll deny every bit of it. You've no proof of anything," Polly said, and sat up in bed.

Fargo strapped his gun belt on and paused at the door. "Don't press your luck, lady," he growled, and hurried from the room and down the stairs. He went out the front door, where the Ovaro still waited at the hitching post; he untied the horse and led the animal down the street.

Dawn had already touched the sky with gray-pink streaks, and when he reached the sheriff's office, he went through a narrow alleyway to the rear, knocked on the door, and waited till Bill Bixby's sleepy face appeared.

"Christ, do you know what time it is?" Bixby grumbled as he let him in.

"Time to get up for you and get some sleep for me," Fargo said. "But we talk first." He sank down in the chair and began to speak in quick, terse sentences, starting with his visit to the warehouse and ending with his visit to Polly. He left out nothing and heard Bixby's sharp gasp of breath as he told of the admissions he'd wrung from Polly. When he finished he sat back, weary from just the telling of it.

"I'll be goddamned," Bixby breathed in awe. "Everybody's friendly banker was a silent partner in a whorehouse, gambling den, and smuggling stolen government goods. Talk about masks. Mr. Respected was really Mr. Crook."

"He made himself a cover nobody would suspect."

"It's a hell of a story, Fargo," Bixby said, awe still in his voice. "But it doesn't answer the damn question. Did Clover Corrigan kill him or didn't she?"

"No," Fargo admitted tersely. "It doesn't answer that."

"But it's getting harder to believe she didn't."

"Go on," Fargo said.

"First, it's damn hard to believe she was his right-hand helper for so long and never knew about this," Bixby began.

"She says he never let her do anything real important," Fargo returned.

"She says a lot of things," Bixby countered. "She says she didn't kill him, but somebody in her red

112

cape ran from Douglas Tremayne's house. She says the cape was stolen and it wasn't her, but you found it at her place and she says whoever stole it put it back. She says Tremayne had a girlfriend, but he was never seen with anybody but her. She says she's staying around to clear her name, but maybe Polly's right about why she didn't run. Maybe she's stayed on to find what she didn't have time to find that night."

"It's still all maybes."

"You don't want to believe it of her," Bixby said with sudden quietness, and Fargo felt the grim smile touch his lips at the younger man's acuity.

"All right," he sighed wearily. "But I want hard proof and I'm going to get it, dammit. Right now I'm wondering if Abbot Tremayne knew this about his favorite younger brother. Maybe that's why he was so quick to offer a reward to have Clover done in."

"It's possible," Bixby murmured, and Fargo wondered silently about Rosalyn. Did she know about Douglas Tremayne's other life? Was that the dirt she feared a trial for Clover would bring out?

"Take the cot," Bixby's voice broke into his thoughts. "I've got to meet the early stage. Sleep as long as you want."

"You can count on that," Fargo said, lowering himself onto the slender cot. He closed his eyes, and his aching, exhausted body embraced sweet sleep before Bixby left the room.

The morning brightness was shut from the room by the drawn shade on the narrow window and the closed door and total weariness let him sleep past the midday mark. When he woke, he washed, dressed, took the time to have a mug of coffee and a hard roll he found, and finally went outside to the waiting horse. He rode from town and sent the Ovaro up into the low hill country, pushing aside all the questions that pulled at him. Speculation was still a pointless exercise, but he realized one thing: in a few days he'd have to ride on to where John Olsen waited with his cattle ready to drive. Maybe, Fargo reflected with grim frustration, the inexorable passage of time and promises to keep would deny him knowing the final truth of it. But he'd keep trying till that moment arrived, near as it was, he promised himself.

He followed the turn in the trail that put him in sight of Abbot Tremayne's house. As he drew closer, an oath exploded from his lips and he put the Ovaro into a gallop. The two figures lay just outside the house, Abbot Tremayne spread-eagled a few feet from the door and Rosalyn crumpled at his side.

Fargo reined up, leapt from the saddle in one motion, and ran the few steps to the front door of the house. The pool of red that engulfed Abbot Tremayne's chest showed that he was past helping, so he went to Rosalyn. She lay on her side, a small trickle of blood almost dry along the side of her temple from a small gash just below the hairline. But she was very much alive, though unconscious, and he saw the shattered pieces of a red clay flower pot alongside her head where she lay.

He lifted her in his arms; she groaned and her eyes flickered open when he carried her into the house and set her down on a leather sofa. He left her there, found the kitchen, and soaked a dish rag with warm water. When he returned to the living room, Rosalyn's eyes were open and they stared almost blankly at him as he knelt down beside her. She continued to stare, then suddenly she exploded in a half-cry, half-gagging gasp and fell against him, her arms clinging tightly around his neck.

"Abbot," she breathed. "Oh, God, Abbot."

"I know," Fargo said, and wiped the blood from her temple. "What happened?"

"I was in the kitchen when I heard Abbot go to the door. Somebody was outside, he said, and went out. The next thing I heard was the shot. I remember I was screaming as I ran from the kitchen. He was lying across the top step, his chest blown in. I ran to him and started to take off my blouse to try to stop the bleeding. I was down beside him when I was hit from behind."

"You didn't see anyone?" Fargo demanded.

"No, but it was her," Rosalyn breathed, her voice almost awestruck.

"How do you know that? You said you didn't see anyone." Fargo frowned.

"Just before I was hit, while I was bending over Abbot, I heard the rustle of calico. I started to turn, but I never made it," Rosalyn said.

"You sure you heard calico?" Fargo pressed.

"No doubt about it. I know the sound. I've plenty of calico blouses and dresses," Rosalyn said, and Fargo got to his feet, his face growing tight.

"First I'll see to your husband," Fargo said.

"No, you've done enough. Just take me into town. I'll get Ephram Sinders to come out and take care of everything. He'll arrange for a service and a proper burial."

"All right," Fargo said, and waited while she went into another room.

When she returned, she'd washed her face, combed the onyx tresses, and changed into a yellow blouse. She led the way out a rear door and took her horse from the corral.

"I'll stay with friends while Ephram Sinders is here. Then I'll come back tonight, after he's finished," Rosalyn said.

"There are things I want to tell you about, but they can wait till later," Fargo said.

"Things you found out?" she asked, and he nodded. "We can talk on the way into town."

"No, later," he said without telling her he wanted to be able to watch her more closely than he could on horseback.

"Stay when you come back tonight, Fargo. I don't want to be alone tonight. Maybe I won't have a chance to hear the rustle of calico next time."

"I'll see," Fargo said, and started down the hill country with Rosalyn drawing up beside him.

"What about Clover Corrigan? You can't keep helping her now, not after this," Rosalyn said.

"I'll think some more on it."

Rosalyn's liquid eyes were wide, a hint of hurt in her voice. "You're wondering if I imagined hearing the rustle of calico. Well, I didn't," she said firmly. "Besides, no one but her had a reason to kill Abbot. She had to stop his offering reward money to have her hunted down."

Fargo nodded, his mouth a thin line. It all made sense. Plain logic made Clover the number-one suspect, and he didn't disbelieve Rosalyn about having heard the rustle of calico. But something bothered him about all of it, a nagging uncertainty he couldn't pin down, some small detail that refused form or definition. He grunted silently and pushed aside the irksome thorn inside him and concentrated on reaching Two Forks Corners while the day was still with him.

When they reached the town, Rosalyn paused as she started down a side street. "Ephram Sinders's place is down here. You go on and I'll be waiting tonight," she said, pleading and promise in the liquid brown eyes.

He nodded and rode on through town. Polly, standing outside her place, watched him ride past with ice in her eyes. The sheriff's office bore a CLOSED sign on the door, and Fargo hurried on out of town. He headed along the flatland and entered the forest, keeping a steady pace, and dusk was dropping over the land when he reached the log cabin tucked away in the depths of the forest.

Clover was about to carry a bucket of water into the house and halted as he rode to a hard stop. Her pert face eyed him warily. "Riding up like that must mean you've found out something," she ventured.

"It does. I found out a lot about your late boss," Fargo said, and swung to the ground. "I'll tell you about it, but then maybe you know all about it already."

Her glower was instant. "What's that supposed to mean?"

"Douglas Tremayne, Mr. Lovable, was a damn fraud. He played the role when he was really a damn, money-grabbing crook," Fargo said. His eyes stayed hard on Clover as he recounted everything he had learned, and he watched for any fleeting expression that might say far more than words. But he saw nothing except her eyes growing wider as he talked, and when he finished, she stared at him, a tiny furrow under the swept-back hair.

"My God," she breathed, awe in her voice.

"And you didn't know a thing about any of this?" Fargo asked.

"No, not a thing," Clover said.

"You never heard or saw a damn thing," Fargo pressed.

"I told you, he only had me doing unimportant details," Clover said. "But don't you see, that explains it. They all believe I know something. They think I've information I don't have. They think I know everything when I don't know anything."

"That's going to take a lot of believing, seeing as how you were his right-hand girl for so long," Fargo commented, and saw Charlie Timkins appear at the door of the cabin.

"You saying you don't believe me, either?" Clover snapped.

"I'm saying you're asking a lot of folks," he told her.

"Well, you can go and believe whatever you want, along with the others," Clover answered, and managed to sound hurt as well as angry.

"One thing more," Fargo said casually, but his eyes peered hard at her. "Abbot Tremayne was murdered this afternoon."

Clover's lips fell open and she stared back at him. "What else are you saying?" she prodded tensely.

"You tell me," Fargo said.

"You saying I did it?" Clover snapped, her eyes blazing.

"You could have. Where were you all day?" he asked.

"Right here. Washing clothes," Clover said.

Fargo's eyes went past her to the old man in the doorway. "That so?" he questioned sharply.

Charlie Timkins met the penetration of his glance for a long moment before answering. "Saw her right here with my own eyes," the old man replied, and turned into the cabin in a gesture of dismissal.

"You've got your damn nerve, Fargo," Clover hissed.

"Words aren't enough anymore. You're too quick with them," Fargo said. He saw some of the anger go from her eyes and she came to him.

"You staying?" she asked, and he shook his head. "Rosalyn Tremayne again?" she snapped waspishly. "You're becoming awfully chummy with her."

"I'm still trying to get at the truth. It could save your neck, remember? Maybe she can help."

"I know. I'm sorry I get angry at you," Clover said, and leaned against him, the high, round breasts pushing up over the neckline of her blouse. "I just want you to stay the night. How's that for honesty?"

"Very good. Soon as I can," Fargo said. "But I'm running out of time, honey."

"You've found out a lot. I'm sure you'll find the truth of it," Clover said, and brushed his lips with a quick kiss. She spun away and hurried into the cabin.

Fargo climbed into the saddle and started to ride through the darkness, picking his way carefully in the almost pitch-black forest. He let his thoughts tumble over each other as he rode.

Clover had been at the cabin all day and that

made motivation and logic meaningless. But Rosalyn insisted she had heard the rustle of calico just before she was struck with the flower pot. Opposites that didn't fit. As he left the forest and started into the hill country, he realized he was still bothered by something about Abbot Tremayne's murder. Something still poked at him, something that still eluded definition but stayed, like a nagging toothache. Perhaps there was something Rosalyn had left out, and he decided to go over it with her again. He quickened his pace as the moon rose to offer a pale light.

When he reached the house, he saw the lamplight in the living room. Rosalyn opened the door as he dismounted and started up the few steps. She wore a filmy nightgown that clearly revealed every curving line of her breasts, her long waist, and her shapely legs. She leaned into him and the soft warmth of her pressed through the nightgown.

"Thanks for coming back," Rosalyn murmured.

"I've things to talk about, things to tell you," Fargo said, and she nodded, stepped back, and drew him down the hall to her room at the far end. She lowered herself onto the edge of the bed and turned a lamp half on, and her liquid brown eyes waited. "Douglas Tremayne was a damn fraud," Fargo began harshly, and her round, brown eyes grew wide at once. He continued and told her everything he had learned, and when he finished, Rosalyn stared into space until she finally broke the silence.

"It seems unbelievable," she murmured. "Simply unbelievable." She brought her eyes to him. "Maybe it's all a pack of lies."

"I saw the stolen government goods myself," Fargo said. "Besides, everything else fits, including why so many people want Clover Corrigan dead for their own reasons. She says she never knew about any of it."

"Of course she'd say that. She's lying. That's why she didn't take my offer and run and why she had to kill Abbot so he'd stop offering rewards for her. She wants time to find what she didn't have a chance to find at Douglas' that night."

"She didn't kill Abbot. She was at a cabin all day. She's got somebody who backed her on it."

"Then they're both lying," Rosalyn said, and came forward to slip her arms around Fargo's neck. "No more talk. It's all so upsetting, so terrible. Just hold me. I want to forget everything that's happened."

"Just one thing: tell me again about this afternoon, exactly how it happened," Fargo said.

Rosalyn shrugged, stepped back, and retold the account she'd given him. When she finished, she had changed nothing and the retelling had triggered no new thoughts in his mind. Fargo swore inwardly. But the undefined still stabbed at him as Rosalyn's arms came around his neck again. Her lips found his mouth, open, wet, and hungrily eager.

"Make the world go away, Fargo," she breathed. "Make it be just you and I." She wriggled her shoulders and the nightgown fell away. Her long, lovely breasts were nakedly beautiful against him, their warmth stirring his loins at once. Her fingers were pulling at his shirt buttons and he kept his mouth closed over hers as he began to shed clothes. Her breasts touched his naked chest in moments, an electric, exciting sensation, and as she fell back onto the bed, Rosalyn kicked off the nightgown and lifted her legs upward and out, the gesture one of wanting and offering, submission and dictation.

"Take me, Fargo," Rosalyn breathed. "Oh, God, take me." He felt his own excitement spiraling as she lifted her torso and her lovely legs pushed apart still farther. Rosalyn quivered, her tight-curled nap trembling, and he sank down on top of her, between the lovely legs and into the smooth vise of desire that instantly closed around him.

Rosalyn groaned when he slid slowly into her waiting warmth and the groan became a low moan as he drew back and came forward again. His mouth found her breasts and he pulled on each one in rhythm with his slow thrustings, and Rosalyn almost growled in pleasure. She pushed with him, drawing her hips back and forth, and her low moaning sounds were cries of sheer animal pleasure. Once again, the thin streak of white in the onyx tresses seemed a flash of lightning against the black thunderclouds of her hair as her head tossed back and forth. "Ah . . . ah . . . aaaagh," Rosalyn suddenly growled, a deep scream that remained cloaked in its own dark ecstasy as her legs tightened around him and she half-rose into the air with her torso, her back arching. "Aaaagh, Jesus, now, now . . . ah, now," Rosalyn cried out, and he felt her quivering contractions surround him, encompassing every part of him as she spiraled to a climax of absolute pleasure.

When her growling cries dwindled away, she sank back on the bed and her sigh was a long, low, shuddering sound. "God, Fargo, we belong together. We could do so many things, you and I," she said.

"You help me reach that place in the Magazine Mountains and you'll never regret a minute of it."

"I've a promise to keep only a day away. I'm going to have to keep it, honey," Fargo said.

She curled against him and stroked his face with one hand. "We'll talk more about that," she said.

He made no reply, content to let her delude herself. It wasn't the time nor the place for arguing; his hand reached down and pushed slowly through the tight-curled triangle, and Rosalyn groaned. Her thighs moved at once and he reached lower and felt her flowing response come with eager instant ardor.

"Yes, yes," Rosalyn growled, and her low voice began to tremble. She turned, brought her thighs over onto him, and sought him at once. She pushed down over him, half-turned, and her hands clasped around his buttocks and pulled him onto her, pushing him in deep, and she gave a moaning scream of delight.

He made love to her again and Rosalyn responded with a ferocity that turned that final moment into an explosion of ecstasy. Finally she lay breathing heavily alongside him across the bed. "You're wonderful," she murmured. "I can't let you go."

"Maybe I can circle back sometime," Fargo said, and she shook the onyx hair.

"No. You've got to stay, go with me," she said. She pressed against him and a night wind suddenly blew in through the half-open window and he felt her shiver. "I'll get a robe," she said, and started to move to pull herself across him.

"I'll get it," he said, and swung long legs from the edge of the bed.

"In the closet by the lamp, the pink robe," Rosalyn said, and sat up on the bed and stretched in contentment. Fargo took three long steps to the closet, pulled the door open, and his eyes moved across an assortment of clothes hanging from their wooden hangers. He spied the pink robe at the end, reached for it, and stepped around three pairs of slippers on the closet floor. Three pairs and one single slipper, he frowned, staring down. The single slipper seemed suddenly to shimmer and glow with a light of its own. Blue, with a red bow, Fargo murmured inside himself, and Clover's description throbbed in his mind. He continued to stare down at it, frozen in place until he shook himself, picked up the single slipper, and brought it from the closet as he tossed the robe to Rosalyn.

"One of a kind?" he asked, holding up the slipper.

"Hardly. There's another one somewhere. I don't know where I put it, but I can't seem to find it," Rosalyn said.

"Try Douglas Tremayne's closet," Fargo growled, and he had his answer in the instant of unguarded surprise and panic that flooded her face. Rosalyn's lips hung open as she stared at him, aware that she had already lost the moment for quick recovery. "It was you," Fargo said, aware of the incredulousness in his voice. "You were the woman. You were having an affair with your husband's brother. I'll be goddammed."

He saw her lips tighten and she swung from the bed, wrapping the robe around her. "All right," she said. "It's true. I did have an affair with Douglas."

"And you took me in with all that bullshit about not having had a man in three years," Fargo said, his voice hardening in anger. "I don't like to be played for a fool, honey."

She came to him, her hands flattening against his chest. "I didn't play you for a fool. I wanted you. Good God, wasn't that plain enough in bed?" she protested.

"Maybe you're just so horny any bull will do," Fargo rasped.

"No, don't think that."

"I'm thinking a lot more than that, honey," Fargo said grimly.

Her liquid black-brown eyes seemed to grow deeper and rounder as she turned from him, her hands clenched together. "You're thinking maybe I killed him," she said.

"Go to the head of the class, baby," Fargo snapped harshly. "You were his secret lover. You could've known everything about him. Maybe you wanted some of the loot he'd been salting away and shot him when he turned you down. You could've arranged it so Clover Corrigan would be blamed for it."

"I never knew anything about that part of Douglas' life. We had an affair and that's what I was afraid would be brought out if she were put on trial. That's why I was willing to help her get away," Rosalyn said, and turned back, lifting her head high and meeting his harsh gaze. "Yes, I was his lover, but being a lover isn't being a killer. Being one doesn't mean being the other."

"No, not just like that it doesn't," Fargo agreed. "But let's say that right now you're suddenly in the running, sister."

"Clover Corrigan killed him and she killed Abbot. She's the only one with reason to do that," Rosalyn said. "You have to believe me, Fargo."

"Dammit, I don't have to believe anything," Fargo barked. "I told you, she's in the clear on Abbot." He brushed past her and pulled on clothes as the anger churned inside him. He wanted only to get away from Rosalyn Tremayne and see if he could sort the truth out of words, more words, explanations, and denials.

"Will you come back, Fargo?" Rosalyn asked.

"Depends," Fargo grunted.

"Come back, please. I need you," Rosalyn said as he strode from the room and he felt the sense of wonder inside him. Her pleas ignored everything he'd said to her, the accusations that painted her as a possible murderess. Was she that arrogantly confident or was it the faith of the innocent? Still wondering, he climbed onto the Ovaro and sent the horse down through the darkened hills. He rode with the churning inside him: suddenly lovely, warm, caring Rosalyn had become a liar, a two-timing little cheat and a thoroughly self-centered little bitch. Was she also a murderess? The question hung in midair and mocked his anger. She had every motivation and opportunity that had been blamed on Clover. Maybe more, he grunted. Maybe love rejected could be added to the others. Yet it all still added up to maybes, a case constructed on possibilities, just as it had with Clover. He increased the horse's pace under the pale moon, anxious to reach the bottom of the hills and go on to Two Forks Corners. He felt frustrated and angry and, worst of all, used. He hadn't brought any of the caution and skepticism to Rosalyn he'd maintained with Clover and suddenly it seemed he'd been very wrong. He swore into the darkness as he reached the level land and sent the horse streaking toward town.

He and Bill Bixby had agreed to share their findings, but more important, it was all going to be in the young sheriff's lap in another twenty-four hours. Once again, it was near dawn when he pounded on the back door of the sheriff's office and saw Bixby's half-asleep face peer out.

"Don't you ever come calling at normal hours?" Bixby muttered as he opened the door.

"Sorry, but I've news you'll want to hear. It'll wake you up, too," Fargo said, and quickly recounted what he had discovered with Rosalyn.

When he finished, Bill Bixby ran a hand through his hair and gave a low whistle. "Damn. This thing takes more turns and twists than a possum's trail," the younger man said, and shot Fargo a sidelong glance. "You're not telling me you think this takes Clover Corrigan off the hook, are you?" he asked.

"No, I can't say that, but it puts a new face on things," Fargo answered.

"Not as much as you'd like it to," Bixby speared, and Fargo shot him a sour glance. "Somebody killed Abbot Tremayne and bashed Rosalyn on the head. Little Clover still had the reasons and chance to do it."

"And an alibi."

Bixby shrugged. "That still doesn't make Rosalyn Tremayne guilty of killing her lover. She was right on that, Fargo. Being a lover doesn't mean she's a killer."

"No, it doesn't, dammit, but it sure doesn't make

her Miss Sweet and Innocent, either," Fargo shot back.

"Guess not," Bixby admitted.

"It's all yours after tomorrow. I'm going to keep my word to John Olsen and break trail for his cattle drive. And you know something, I'm going to be damn glad to get on with it," Fargo said.

Bixby smiled. "Don't blame you. I'll stay on it as soon as I get back."

"Get back?" Fargo frowned.

"Got word that the sheriff in Albarville picked up a sidewinder we want for gunning down a rancher. I'm going to bring him back. Be gone only a few days."

"I'll catch a few hours of shut-eye on your cot," Fargo said, and removed his gun belt to sit down on the edge of the narrow bed.

"Go ahead," Bixby said. "You going to stop by when your drive's over to find out what happened?"

Fargo considered the question for a moment. "Not likely," he said. "Think maybe I'd rather not know."

The younger man nodded and finished dressing. "Might be best that way," he agreed. "I'll try to be sure I bring in the right one."

"Thanks," Fargo said, closed his eyes, and heard Bill Bixby leave the little room.

He allowed himself to sleep until midday, and when he rose, he used the basin of cold water on the floor to wash. He went outside, climbed onto the Ovaro, and slowly rode into the main street, past the gaming house, and he remembered Bill Bixby's warning as he did so. But Ed Dooley's place was closed and he saw no one watching him as he passed the dance hall. He drew abreast of the general store, idly glanced at the window, and suddenly pulled the pinto to a halt. His eyes stayed fixed on the store window and the frown came to slide across his brow. A half-dozen small wooden doll figures lined one corner of the window and he read the sign wedged in alongside them.

NEW CARVINGS FROM CHARLIE TIMKINS.
GET THEM WHILE THEY LAST

Fargo stared at the sign and felt rage spiraling inside him. Goddamn, he swore silently, and sent the Ovaro into a gallop. He held the pace, slowed only when he began to thread his way through the forest and increased speed again as he neared the log cabin. He raced to a skidding halt and Charlie Timkins stepped from the doorway. "Where is she?" Fargo barked.

"Went to the pond to have herself a bath."

"We're going to talk, old man," Fargo said, and loomed over Charlie Timkins in three long-legged strides, his eyes blazing blue fire. "I saw your figures in the general store. You had to deliver them yesterday," he barked, and saw the old man's eyes blink nervously. Charlie Timkins looked away and half-shrugged. "How long were you away, goddammit?" Fargo roared.

The old man shrugged again. "It takes a spell just getting to town and back, and I always stay to talk some with Herb Atkins," he said.

"How long, dammit?" Fargo roared again.

"Most of the day, I guess," he said.

"Why'd you lie to me about Clover being here?" Fargo pressed angrily. "Why'd you say you saw her here with your own eyes?"

129

"I did. She was here when I left. It wasn't a real lie," the old man protested.

"Enough of one, damn your old hide," Fargo snapped.

"I told him to back me up," Clover's voice cut in, and Fargo whirled, one hand on his gun instantly. She came through the brush, a towel over one arm and tiny droplets of water still on her pert face. "I knew you'd only go thinking the wrong thing, just as you are right now," she flung at him.

"You're goddamn right," Fargo returned. "You had most of the day alone. You could've done it. You had plenty of time."

"Only I didn't. I was right here," she said.

"More words. Maybe more lies," Fargo blazed. "You got that old man to lie for you this time around." Clover's eyes narrowed and she stared back at him. "Well, I'm finished, honey. I wanted to believe in you. Hell, I tried, but I'm all out of believing in smooth words and fast answers. Maybe you didn't do it and maybe you did. I don't much care anymore. Come morning, I'm going to John Olsen and keep my word to him."

"You can't do that, Fargo. You can't just walk out on me now. You're coming close to the truth. You can't just leave," she said.

He frowned incredulously at her. "Damn, you haven't lost any of your brass, have you?"

She came to him and her pert face softened. "I haven't stopped being grateful to you, but you can't just give up on me now," she said. "I didn't kill anybody. Stay the night. I can convince you again, Fargo."

"Forget it, honey," he snapped. "I want proof, not pussy."

"Then stay on and help me prove to you that I didn't do it," Clover said.

"I'm out, honey. Do your own proving if you can. I've had enough," Fargo shot back.

"You can't walk away now. I won't let you."

"Clover, honey, there's not a damn thing you can do about that," he said, and met the glower she tossed at him. He left her standing beside the log cabin, the glower following him as he rode away, and he cursed at himself for the pang of guilt that ran through him. She still had the ability to do that, damn her pert hide. But she'd always been too quick with answers. She remained an appealing enigma and he'd leave it to Bill Bixby to get at the truth of it. It all put a sour taste in his mouth now, and he hurried through the forest and into the hill country. He had one thing to put straight before taking off.

Dusk had begun to descend when he pulled up at Rosalyn's house. She hurried out to meet him, the liquid eyes searching his face.

"Came to tell you that I might owe you an apology," Fargo said, swinging out of the saddle. "Clover Corrigan's alibi for where she was yesterday didn't hold up. Maybe you did hear that rustle of calico."

"Of course I did," Rosalyn said with just an edge of triumph. "You'll stay now and help me prove it?" she asked.

"No, afraid not," he said. "I've a cattle drive to lead, come morning."

"Then we'll forget about Clover. Let her live with her killings. Just help me get away from it all. Take me into the Magazine Mountains, Fargo. I need you for that. I'll need the very best, I told you, and that's you, in so many ways." She came to him and offered her mouth to him, but he only peered down at her.

"Sorry, honey," he said coldly as he forced himself to remember that despite what he'd found out about Clover's lies, Rosalyn had lied and cheated through her affair and to him. Innocence was a mask she wore well. She'd had plenty of practice.

She snapped back at his refusal and her eyes narrowed. "You're my tomorrows, Fargo. I need you."

"Life's full of disappointments, honey."

"Not for me. I don't accept disappointments," Rosalyn said very quietly.

"There's always a first time," Fargo returned, and pulled himself onto the pinto. "I just wanted to tell you I was wrong about her alibi. Figured I owed you that," he said.

"Thank you," Rosalyn answered.

He turned the horse and rode away, not glancing back. He didn't need to, for she stayed with him as he rode, the stunning quality of her and the deep beauty of those liquid eyes. They each had their ways of proclaiming innocence—Clover with injured indignation, Rosalyn with slow-eyed softness—and he wondered as he rode if perhaps they were both innocent. Perhaps the killer was someone else entirely. Perhaps he had spent too much time thinking about Clover and Rosalyn. The town madam had proved she thought nothing of ordering him killed. And Douglas Tremayne had lived his own secret life. Perhaps he had encouraged someone else's wrath, Fargo pondered, someone not even in the picture.

He swore and threw away the thought. The killer had to be a part of the small circle surrounding Douglas Tremayne, someone who knew how, where, and when to strike. And perhaps to use a red cape to plant the blame. Perhaps, Fargo grunted. Perhaps the red cape had never been worn by anyone except its owner. It was all still too full of maybes, he muttered inwardly, and he was glad to leave it behind.

He reached the base of the low hills, turned northwest, and found a spot to bed down. He wanted one good night's sleep before starting to break trail for the cattle drive, and he set out his bedroll and let the night sweep away all but slumber.

The sun had stretched warm fingers across the land when he woke. He found a stream, washed, breakfasted on wild pears, and slowly turned the pinto northward. He had vowed not to think any longer about the masks of lovely young women, and he sent the pinto northward into land that brought gentle hills and where the rockbound hardness grew softer. He climbed the top of a rise and saw the ranch below, the herd grazing free on a wide stretch of good fescue grass.

He took the pinto down the slope toward the ranchhouse. The cowhands gathered there didn't surprise him, but he frowned at the number of buggies that filled the front yard. He took in buckboards, surreys, runabouts, canvas-roofed phaetons, and one fixed-top Brunswick. He reined up outside the house, dismounted, and passed a woman and a man leaving, both grim-faced, the woman dabbing at her eyes with a handkerchief. A man in his late twenties, Fargo guessed, met him at the door.

"Name's Fargo, Skye Fargo. I'm here to see John Olsen," Skye said.

"Fargo . . . the Trailsman," the man said, and Fargo nodded. "I'm Zeke. I'm John Olsen's son."

"My pleasure," Fargo said, and cast a glance at the number of buggies in the yard. "All these folks come to wish you luck on your drive?" he asked.

"No, they're all family friends," Zeke Olsen said. "My pa was killed at the crack of dawn this morning."

"Killed?" Fargo frowned in shock.

"He came out of the house to check on the herd as he always does. Someone was waiting for him and killed him with one shot, just gunned him down," the young man said. "There won't be any cattle drive now. We've praying, burying and talking to do."

Fargo knew he was staring at the young man and the words he had just heard flamed inside him, throbbing, afire with a sudden life of their own: "My pa was killed. . . . There won't be any cattle drive now."

7

Fargo was aware of the man frowning at him as he stared with shock flooding his face. He was transfixed in his own world and only Zeke Olsen's voice snapped him out of it. "I'm sorry, Fargo. We'll pay you for your time coming here."

"No, please, that won't be necessary. That's not what I was thinking about," Fargo said. "Your pa have any enemies?"

"No. Nobody was even annoyed with him. It all happened out of the blue. Some folks are thinking that maybe it was some kind of mistake," Zeke Olsen said. "That's the only way we can explain it."

"Yes, maybe," Fargo muttered, and turned away, his jaw throbbing as he climbed onto the pinto.

"We'll be in touch again, Fargo, soon as we're ready to go on and Pa's at peace," Zeke Olsen called.

"I'm sorry for what happened," Fargo told the young man. He slowly moved out of the front yard, his lips a tight, grim line, his thoughts spilling over one another. He'd no blame for what had happened to poor John Olsen. Reason and logic told him that. Yet he felt as though he shared the blame, and his heart and soul told him that. He hadn't seen what he perhaps should have seen. He had underestimated the icy depths of ruthless determination. The words spiraled invisibly back to him and his lips pulled back in grim distaste: "You can't walk away now. I won't let you." Those were Clover's words and he'd dismissed them as nothing more. "I don't accept disappointments," Rosalyn had said to him, and again he'd taken them as only hollow talk.

But he had been wrong, Fargo swore silently as he rode. Wrong about one of them, and an innocent man lay dead. He cursed again and pulled the Ovaro into a glen where the sassafras grew thick. He dismounted and stretched out on a bed of nut moss. Clover or Rosalyn? he muttered. One of them made certain he'd not lead a cattle drive. One of them was a clever, ruthless, and cold-blooded murderess, a killer in calico. But which one? He grimaced. Slowly and carefully, he began to review every detail he knew in his mind, weighing each one, sifting through all the answers and explanations, searching for something that would shape itself into a certain answer. The sun rose high and slid into the afternoon sky when he finally sat up and cursed in angry frustration. He could find nothing that gave him that last measure of certainty.

Something about Abbot Tremayne's murder still bothered Fargo and still remained undefined. But that was the only piece that didn't fit into place. All the others formed their patterns and all were infuriatingly alike. He was going around in circles, he realized, just as he had from the very start of it. Guilt and innocence pointed at both with equal insistence. But one was like a Venus's-flytrap, masking deadliness with beauty, and he knew there was only one way to the truth now. He had to make deadliness reveal itself; he had to trigger proof. One of them had stopped the cattle drive from taking him away. One of them expected he'd return, still curious to pursue truth. One of them was certain she could turn it all her way.

Fargo almost smiled as his plans took shape. If the cattle drive went on, if he didn't return, one of them would come looking, driven by curiosity and the need to try again. The one who came would be the calico killer, the one who had added innocent John Olsen to her list of killings.

Clover or Rosalyn? he wondered bitterly and turned away from even hazarding a guess now. He rose, clambered onto the Ovaro, and turned back northward to the Olsen ranch. Night had come when he reached the ranch house, where one lamp burned inside one of the windows. A black ribbon had been fixed onto the front door, he observed as he knocked. Zeke Olsen and a younger man opened the door, and Fargo saw the surprise on Zeke's face.

"Sorry to bother you at a time like this," Fargo said. "But it's now or never."

"What's now or never?" Zeke said.

"To find out who killed your pa," Fargo answered, and both men stared at him. "I thought you'd want to know that."

"Come in, Fargo," Zeke said. "This is my brother, Jed."

Jed speared him with a wary glance as he stepped into the quiet house. "How would you be knowing anything about who killed my pa, Fargo?" he asked.

"It's a long story and I'll skip all the details," Fargo said, and they listened with frowns of astonishment as he sketched in the broad outlines.

It was the younger brother who spoke first when he finished. "We'll do whatever you want, Fargo. I want this bitch, whichever one it is, to pay for killing Pa. You need men to hunt her down, you've got them."

"Can't hunt down a question mark," Fargo said. "I want you to let me take the herd out, just as if you were going on with the drive. Get the word out that that's what you're doing."

"All right," Zeke Olsen said.

"I'll only want about a quarter of your hands to go along. Tell them they'll get their orders from me."

"Consider it done," Zeke said.

"That's all I'll need. I'll play out the rest of it," Fargo said. "Tell your men to be ready, come morning."

"The bunkhouse is full but we've a spare room you can use for the night," Zeke Olsen offered.

"Thanks, but I've things to do first. I'll bed down somewhere and be here in the morning," Fargo answered, and the two men walked from the house with him. They watched as he rode away.

Fargo turned the Ovaro west under the moon, which had risen to paint the land with a silver patina. He rode on, his eyes scanning the terrain, just as he would do were the drive really to take place. The flatland stretched out ahead of him, low hills to the left and, at the base of them, a good, thick stand of forest. He rode on for perhaps an hour until he had seen enough and then turned back, found a place to bed down, and let the remainder of the night pass in sleep. But his thoughts continued to turn of themselves and the night was still dark when he suddenly woke and sat up. The slow smile that touched his lips was edged with grimness. The one irksome, nagging thing about Abbot Tremayne's murder was no longer an undefined question, and as he sank back onto his bedroll, Fargo made a wager with himself before he returned to sleep.

When the morning sun woke him, he washed, dressed and made his way to the Olsen place. A woman garbed in widow's black watched from the window as he began to lead the herd slowly from their grazing stand near the house. Zeke Olsen introduced him to five cowhands, all leathered men with experience in their eyes and in the easy way they went about riding herd.

Fargo rode ahead and let the men handle the steers. He surveyed the land he'd ridden by moonlight. The line of forest stayed all along the base of the hills, going on as far as he could see, mostly hawthorn and box elder with some blackjack oak. When the day drew near an end, he returned to the herd and motioned to the cowhands. "Bring them close up to the trees," he said. "Let them settle down for the night there."

The herders began to move the steers in to the edge of the forest and darkness settled down. Fargo waited for the men to eat their supper meal and approached them when they were finished. "Come dawn, I want you to disappear, go back into the trees if you want or out along the flatland. Go off as far as you can and still stay in sight of the herd so when I wave you back you'll see me," he said.

"Got it," one of the men said. "Zeke told us we'd be turning back in time."

"Soon as I get the visitor I expect," Fargo said.

The men nodded and kept any more questions to themselves.

Fargo turned away and found a spot only a few yards from the edge of the trees to set out his bedroll. He stretched out and watched one of the cowhands take nightwatch around the far periphery of the herd. The steers held calm with only the usual deep mooing. He dropped off to sleep, but not before he thought again of the wager he'd made with himself. The morning would bring the answer, he was all but certain, and he slept with the big Colt beside his hand. Not that he expected that kind of trouble. But final moves could bring final surprises. It was a time for caution.

When the night finally fled before the morning sun, he woke, sat up, and used his canteen to wash. He dressed and peered into the distance, where he spotted the small knot of figures on the flatland. He found a mulberry tree and breakfasted on the sweet fruit. When he finished, he gave the pinto a cursory grooming with the body brush from his saddlebag. He climbed onto the horse and stayed quietly in the saddle. He would ordinarily have heard the figure came from the trees, but the steers made just enough noise to cover the sound of slow hoofbeats and the crack of twigs and suddenly the horse and rider were there, halted but a few feet away.

He felt the wryness in the grim smile that edged his lips as he looked across at the pert face and the very round, high bust. "I just lost a bet," he said. "But then you've been a package of surprises all along. Maybe I should've expected one more."

"What are you talking about?" Clover frowned.

"Your being here, that's what," Fargo said, his voice hardening.

"I came for a last try to get you to help me," she said.

"Did you?" Fargo returned. "Or did you come because you couldn't believe what you heard? Did you come because you had to see for yourself?"

"I don't know what you're talking about," Clover snapped.

"Yes, she does, and that's exactly why she's here," a voice cut in, and Fargo turned in the saddle to see Rosalyn ride out of the trees. Goddamn, he swore silently as surprise stabbed into him again. "She expected there wouldn't be any cattle drive and she came to see for herself."

Fargo's eyes narrowed. "How about you, Rosalyn? What are you doing here?" he asked.

"I came to raise my offer and get you to go back with me," Rosalyn said, and turned the round, liquid eyes on him.

"Did you? I'm thinking maybe I didn't lose that bet with myself," Fargo said. "How'd you know Clover expected there'd be no cattle drive?"

A tiny furrow dug into Rosalyn's smooth brow. "You were just talking to her about that," she answered.

"Good try, honey, but not good enough. I asked her a question, but I hadn't spelled out anything. There was no way for you to know what she expected, except one. You knew because that's what you expected: no cattle drive."

"I don't know what you mean," Rosalyn said, but he had caught the moment of apprehension that flashed through her face.

"The hell you don't, honey. You know because you made it happen, all of it, from the very beginning. You tripped yourself up just now by telling me what Clover expected," Fargo rasped.

"You've gone mad. This little tramp has turned your head soft," Rosalyn flung back.

"No, but I'll admit you had me fooled for most of it. You stole her red cape and set her up and figured that lynch mob would take care of everything. But I stopped that. You were happy to see Dandridge's men take her because you knew she couldn't tell them anything and they'd kill her for it anyway. But I came along again."

"Yes, and I helped you rescue her. Where does that fit with your wild story?" Rosalyn shot back.

"It didn't, but then I came to realize you'd been really clever then. You knew I'd get to them even without your help. This way you got me to bring her back and you tried to ship her off, the selfless gesture. You figured she'd take it and that'd get her out of your hair and she'd stay the guilty one who'd run off. Only Clover didn't go for it and so you began to cosy up to me to make sure I eased up on helping her."

"Go to hell, Fargo," Rosalyn snapped.

"You decided killing your husband and blaming Clover would finish my wondering about her. It almost did, too, especially with all the boneheaded things Clover did. But something about that kept bothering me. I couldn't pin it down until last night. A killer wouldn't kill one victim and hit the other on the head with a flower pot. Clover would've blasted you away, too, had she killed Abbot. You killed your husband and then knocked yourself out with the flower pot. Then you gave me that story about the rustle of calico." He paused and saw Rosalyn's liquid eyes had become pools of black hate. "Douglas Tremayne had hidden all his loot somewhere in the Magazine Mountains, hadn't he? You found that much out. That's what you wanted me to help you find out there," Fargo finished.

"You put a lot of little things together, didn't you, Fargo?" Rosalyn said, her low, purring voice now a deep hiss.

"It took me a spell, too long, I guess. But better late than never."

"The word is never, Fargo," Rosalyn said, and he saw her bring her hand down sharply on her horse's rump. He'd half-expected her to try to run, but she sent the horse directly at Clover and he saw her arm reach out, smash into Clover, and send the girl flying from the saddle.

Fargo spun the Ovaro around to the other side as Clover's mount pulled forward, but he reined up as he saw Rosalyn with one hand holding Clover by the hair, the other pointing a big Allen and Wheelock army revolver at her head.

"Back away, Fargo, or I'll blow her head off," Rosalyn said, and Fargo backed the Ovaro at once.

"Don't do anything stupid, Rosalyn," Fargo said.

"I'd follow that advice if I were you," she snapped back. He saw her yank Clover's head up and heard Clover's yelp of pain. "Climb on into the saddle in front of me, darling," Rosalyn purred at Clover, and Fargo watched as Clover carefully pulled herself onto the horse. Rosalyn let go of her grip on Clover's hair but kept the six-shot Wheelock tight into the girl's back. "Now, Fargo, you drop your gun. Nice and slow or I'll blow her back apart," Rosalyn Tremayne warned. "You know I'll do it, Fargo."

"Yes, I know it," Fargo growled, and carefully lifted the Colt from his holster and let it drop to the ground.

"Now, you stay right where you are, Fargo," Rosalyn said. "Don't move an inch in any direction." Her eyes staying on him, she began to move her horse through the herd, pushing her way past the steers, and he saw the animals move restlessly. She continued on right into the center of the herd and her eyes stayed on him as she moved the horse forward. She was starting into the thickest knot of steers when he saw her take the gun from Clover's back and level it at him.

"No, don't shoot," Fargo called.

"Your time to go, you meddling bastard," Rosalyn shouted, the gun steady.

"No, you goddamn fool, don't shoot," Fargo shouted, and flung himself sideways from the saddle as the first shot whistled past his ear. He hit the ground and heard the three shots Rosalyn fired in quick succession. Two kicked up dirt only a fraction of an inch from him as he rolled. He also heard the sudden explosion of hooves and the bellows of panic as the steers began to stampede. Like an ocean wave gathering itself, the great mass of bodies began to move, a low rumbling sound at first, and then the earth began to shake. The steers spread, then came together, and aimless panic instantly became a focused charge as they swung in behind the lead bulls at the outer edges.

Fargo pulled himself to his feet, managed to avoid

being sent sprawling by two thundering bodies, and leapt onto the Ovaro. He saw Rosalyn on her horse, still holding Clover in the saddle with her, and saw her trying to pull the horse in a tight circle.

"No, dammit," he shouted, but knew the sound of his voice was drowned out by the pounding of hooves. A dozen thundering steers rushed at him and he turned the Ovaro in the same direction they raced, letting the horse run along with them. He heard a scream, Clover's voice, and saw her fall from the saddle as Rosalyn pushed her away and sent the horse leaping forward. He yanked on the reins, leaned the Ovaro against a steer alongside, and pulled the Sharps from its saddle holster. He fired close to the steer's ear and the animal veered to the left. A half-dozen others went with him, opening a slender path to where Clover lay on the ground. He sent the Ovaro racing forward. Clover rose to one knee and stretched her arms up as he charged past and she caught hold of his reaching arms.

"Hang on," he said, and Clover's arms fastened around him as he swung her onto the horse. He kept the Ovaro racing forward with the stampeding cattle and spotted Rosalyn a dozen yards ahead. She was still trying to fight her way out of the center of the stampede and he saw her horse knocked sideways and sent stumbling back again as it was hit from the other side.

"No, go with them, dammit, go with them," he shouted, and brought his attention back to his own horse as he felt the steed being wedged in between thundering bodies. "Steady, boy, steady," he shouted, and kept the horse's head up with a firmly soothing, controlled rein. He felt the pinto pick up speed, race between the steers, and keep his footing. As they outraced the steers on either side of them, Clover clung to him, her arms tight around his waist.

A sharp scream cut through the sound of the stampede and Fargo's glance snapped to his right in time to see Rosalyn's form falling to one side as her horse went down. "Oh, Jesus," he muttered as she disappeared behind the wall of brown-and-white hides. He heard her scream again, this time the sound filled with pain.

Clover's face pressed into his chest as Rosalyn's scream came again, a broken sound now, suddenly cut off, and Fargo let the Ovaro go on with a dozen steers that veered off to the left. He listened for Rosalyn Tremayne's voice but the thunder of hooves was all he heard and he found himself thinking of the steady drumbeats of a funeral march. The Ovaro kept veering off with the steers and the pressure against the horse lessened as the cattle began to spread out. Fargo saw the cowhands arriving to race around the periphery of the herd and start to turn the stampede around. Fargo saw an opening, veered, and took the Ovaro to the back edge, where only a dozen steers ran with increasing aimlessness.

He saw another break in the rush of cattle and sent the horse into the clear and reined to a halt.

"Oh, God," Clover said into his ear, still clinging to him. "Oh, God, we're alive." She pulled back and stared up into his eyes, slowly turning her head to gaze across the flatland to where the cowhands in the distance were breaking up the stampede. A fine film of dust rose from the ground, filtered into the air, and blew away.

Fargo peered across the land with her and felt Clover's hands dig into his arms as she took a moment longer to find the torn and red-stained garments that lay flattened across the ground.

"I'm going to be sick," Clover murmured, and turned her head away from the crushed, trampled remains of Rosalyn Tremayne.

Fargo wheeled the Ovaro toward the distant trees and spotted Clover's horse. She trembled as she climbed from him to her horse, and the usually pert and pugnacious face was clouded with somberness.

"Why'd she blame it on me? I never did anything to her," Clover asked.

"She needed a killer and you fitted best," Fargo said, retrieving the Colt.

"She almost pulled it off," Clover murmured.

"Almost doesn't count," Fargo said, and looked past her to where two of the cowhands approached. "You can turn them back now," he told the two men when they halted. "It's over. Tell the Olsens that their pa's killer has paid for it."

One of the men nodded toward the cluster of torn and stained garments. "Not much left, but we'll give you a hand if you want."

"Guess we may as well do the right thing," Fargo said, and cast a glance at Clover. "You wait here," he said, and she nodded. He rode with the two cowhands and helped dig a makeshift, shallow resting place for the woman who had worn her own set of masks, and when he returned to Clover, the sourness rode wit him.

"Let's get away from here, Fargo," Clover said. "I don't want to go back, not tonight."

He nodded and glanced at the afternoon sun,

which began to slide toward the horizon. She rode in silence beside him as he led the way through the trees, staying in the woodland and finally halting just before dusk where a stream babbled its way through the forest silence. He slid from the pinto, helped Clover from her horse, and unsaddled both mounts. Night stole quietly into the woods and he set out his bedroll, shared a stick of cold beef jerky with Clover, and began to undress as the moon filtered through the branches.

He saw her watching him, taking in the hard-muscled beauty of his body as he undressed to the bottoms of his underwear. "You going to stay out there?" he asked as he slid into his bedroll.

"No, damn," she said, and gave a tiny giggle as she flung her shirt off and pulled off the rest of her clothes to stand before him, the high, round, full breasts pushing outward from her compact, sturdy body. With a half-bound, she almost leapt into the bedroll and her arms came around him at once. She moved upward enough to press her breasts into his face and he delighted in their soft firmness as she rubbed them back and forth across his lips, pausing to let him catch first one tiny tip, then the other.

"Oh, Fargo, Fargo," Clover Corrigan breathed as he pulled and sucked on the light-pink little nipples, and her hands pressed hard into his chest. He brought his own hand down across her rounded compact belly, caressing its convex firmness, and moved down to the modest black triangle, pushing his fingers through the soft-wire covering and pressing down on the fleshy little mound underneath. His hand slid lower, probing between the compact flesh of her thighs, and Clover cried out at his touch and he felt her inner thighs already warmly moist with wanting.

He touched, slowly, letting his hand rest against the very edge of her, and she called out, protest and demand in her voice, wanting and pleading mixed in with her pugnacious little self. "Go on, damn you, Fargo . . . oh, Jeeeeez, go on," Clover murmured, and her torso twisted to one side, then the other, and returned to lift itself upward at him. He slid down along the warmth of her inner thighs with his hand and cupped his palm against the dark, moist portal, and she half-screamed in pleasure and pushed forward to press against him. He let his hand stay as she pushed harder against him, and tiny gasps of demand came from her lips. When he moved in to touch the wet, waiting lips, her scream spiraled into the night. "Yes, yes . . . ah, ah, yes," Clover gasped, and the gasp became a groan of pleasure as he pushed deeper, rubbed, caressed, probed the soft, sensitive places that sent her screams of delight following one another in quick succession.

"More, more, oh, damn, more," Clover cried out, and lifted her torso, then fell back onto the bedroll, her legs falling open, straightening, falling open again, and her hand curling around the back of his neck, pulling his mouth down to hers. Her tongue came out to caress his lips and probe deeper into his mouth, an echo of desire, messenger of the flesh, and when she paused to gulp in air, he heard her breath-filled pleas.

"Take me, Fargo, oh, God, take me," Clover murmured, and pushed his face down onto her round, high breasts. Her sturdy, vibrant young legs fell open again, half-twisting to catch at him, pulling, entreating, and he let himself roll over onto her compact body. She gave a short cry of delight as his throbbing, searching maleness came against her. Clover's pubic mound lifted, her body imploring, her senses reaching out for relief, and he lifted himself, bringing his own eagerness to the dark, warm welcome, and slid forward.

"Oh, Oh, Jeeez . . . oh, yes, oh, God, yes," Clover gasped as she began to move with him, sliding her body back and forth in rhythm with his every motion.

She fell into complete oneness with him and at the point of each slow thrust she gave a tiny gasp of delight. As his motions quickened, growing more intense, she stayed with him and the gasps grew louder, became tiny half-screams of joy. When he felt her hands dig into his back and heard her gasps grow more breath-filled, he quickened the pace of pleasure and Clover's voice became a whispered scream. "Yes, now, now, oh, Jeez, I . . . I . . . I'm coming, oh, God," she cried out, and he felt her sturdy legs grow tight around him and her pelvis thrust up. He let his own peak of delight explode with her, and her scream filled the night as she reached that moment of moments—flesh, mind, body, all funneled into one instant of pure ecstasy. Clover hung on to him until she stopped gasping and quivering, crying out tiny sounds and holding his face down to the high, very round breasts. Finally she released her grip on him and lay back, giving a long, satisfied sigh.

"Better than before," he commented as he lay beside her.

"Yes, oh, yes," Clover murmured, and curled

herself against him. He took in the compact, sturdy vibrancy of her, its own kind of beauty, made of youth and vigor and that inner pugnaciousness that was her own special quality. He watched her go to sleep against him, contented as a Cheshire cat, and he closed his eyes and let sweet sleep wrap itself around him too.

When morning came, he felt her warmth still against him, but she moved as he opened his eyes. He glimpsed her bound to her feet and go to the brook and he watched her from one elbow as she washed, lay flat in the swift-running stream, sat up, and rubbed the cool water across her body with both hands. She was too compact and sturdy for the ethereal spriteliness of a wood nymph and not leggy and slender enough to resemble a young colt. She was more the happy puppy full of the pure enjoyment of life and he rose and went to her, lowering himself into the brook and feeling the invigorating coolness of the water as it leapt and lapped at him. Clover watched as he came to her, stayed watching while he reclined in the brook, and she suddenly moved up to him, her hands on his legs, moving up along his thighs and finally, curling her fingers around him.

She began to stroke gently, then harder, and his response was almost instant. "Oh, oh," she murmured as she felt his firmness gather strength and enlarge under her touch. "I've never made love in a brook before," she said, and brought her lips down to him and he felt the shudder of pleasure go through him.

"There's always a first time," he murmured, and she nodded as she continued to enjoy her mouth on him, her lips softly caressing, pulling, taking him in deeply. He felt the wondrous pleasure of her, his body growing hot under her touch, and the cool waters of the brook sent their own sensation along his back, his buttocks, and the back of his legs. The combination of hot and cold sent a shiver of delight through him and he felt himself throbbing, pulsations growing quicker.

"Oh, oh, oh," Clover murmured as she too felt his ecstasy, and he saw her bring her legs up, almost to a kneeling position, and he reached down and gently pulled her lips from him and she was on top of him at once, pushing herself down over him as she exploded in a climax of ecstasy and he with her. She half-screamed and her head came down against his face and she lifted, pressing her breasts into his mouth as she continued to come in quivering, ardent spasms. Finally, with a tremendous sigh, she grew limp, stayed atop him for a long minute, and then fell onto her side, half in the brook and hard against him. "Wow," Clover breathed softly and contentedly. Fargo rolled from the brook and pulled her with him onto the soft haircap moss along the bank and let the warm sun that filtered its way through the dense branches finally dry his skin.

When he rose, Clover murmured in protest but sat up and began to pull on her clothes.

"We'll head back," Fargo said. "You'll be wanting to pick up your things at Charlie Timkins' place." Clover nodded and helped him saddle the horses.

When they were finished, she swung onto her mount and rode alongside him through the woods. They emerged at a stretch of gently rolling land with an occasional hackberry dotting its expanse.

Fargo had just led the way up a hill when a half-dozen horsemen crested the top, reined up, and peered at him.

"Shit," Fargo swore, and recognized Ed Dooley at the head of the riders. The man had spotted them at once and Fargo saw him draw his six-gun and fire a shot into the air. "This way," Fargo rasped at Clover as he spun the pinto around and raced off along the bottom of the slope. He cast a glance up and back and saw Dooley and his posse were racing down the slope after them. "Goddamn," he swore again as another band of riders appeared a few dozen yards directly in front of them, and this time he recognized Cyril Dandridge's tight, weasel face in the forefront.

He veered the pinto to his left and Clover followed as he raced away. He'd gone perhaps a hundred yards when the third posse of horsemen appeared to block his path, and he instantly spotted Polly in the lead. At least another six gunslingers with her, he guessed, and he again sent the pinto in another direction. Bill Bixby's warning returned to him and he swore into the wind. He'd forgotten about it and now he saw the trio had hired a whole passel of gunslingers to hunt him down. He sent the pinto racing into the woods, glanced back to see Clover staying on his heels, and slowed enough for her to catch up when he was into the forest.

"It's over," Clover said. "Why are they chasing us now?"

"We both know too much now," Fargo answered. "We could go back and tell everything we know, and none of them want that."

"I don't give a damn about what they did or didn't do," Clover said. "I just want to leave here."

"They're not going to take a chance on that. They want to make sure you'll keep quiet. The same for me," Fargo said, and veered the Ovaro to the left along a deer trail.

"We going to hide out in here?" Clover asked, and he shook his head as he heard the first of the three posses crashing through the brush behind them.

"They'd hunt us down in here," he said. "I want space to maneuver, but first I want a place to think."

"Where?" she asked, and he shrugged.

"Wherever looks right. But first we'll let them do some chasing," he said, and sent the pinto forward until he reached the other edge of the woodland and raced into the open to find himself on a hillside with stands of red oak scattered across it. He kept the pinto at a steady pace as he crossed diagonally halfway up the hill, looked back, and saw Ed Dooley's band emerge from the woods first, slow, and finally spot him and take off again. Dandridge and his group emerged next and veered off to the left, and finally Polly appeared with her band. She turned sharply to the right and Fargo nodded grimly. Their maneuvers were costing them time and ground, but they wanted to keep him outflanked and boxed in.

"Not yet, cousins," he muttered aloud, and kept the Ovaro at the horse's steady pace.

The pinto could go all day at the pace, he knew, but Clover's mount would never hold up. His eyes scanned the land ahead and on both sides as he rode. Dooley and the others were content to stay following; left to his own, he'd have had them tiring fast and dropping back. But he'd be doing the same keeping Clover with him, and his eyes grew narrow as they scanned the terrain. The hills grew steeper and he saw a half-dozen deep cuts and gorges appear to his left. Slowly, he edged toward the harsher land, and as the afternoon began to slide toward an end, he took a sharp turn up a steep hillside. He slowed, and seeing Clover's mount tiring fast, he halted for a moment on a flat ledge that let him look down and behind. Ed Dooley's posse had slowed perceptibly but they were doggedly staying on his tail. Dandridge's men were far to the right, he saw, looking for a spot to climb upwards, and Polly was out of sight with her posse.

But they were holding to their plan, he saw, and he nodded to Clover and sent the pinto on higher into the hills. He turned again, went through a rock-lined passage, and came out where thick black-jack oak grew amid heavy rock formations. He cast a glance skyward and grunted in satisfaction. This was the land he wanted to find at the time he wanted to reach it, and he nosed the pinto carefully along the passages. He poked through a thick growth of high brush and oak in front of a tall slab of rock and drew to a halt at the mouth of a cave, its entrance tall enough for the horses to fit through.

He entered the dank, musty cave, moving slowly, and drew his rifle from its saddle holster as he smelled the stale odor of bear and possum. The cave held a sharp rock-lined turn that went into a second cave, and he followed it in the near-blackness, halted, and drew his breath in deeply. All the dank and damp odors were stale ones. He dismounted and beckoned to Clover. "You stay here," he said. "See if you can get a small fire going. There are a lot of old, dry twigs in here. Keep it small."

He took the Ovaro back out of the cave and returned to the trail that led past the dense brush and the oaks. He sent the horse onward for perhaps a half-mile, dismounted, and moved into the thick brush. He pushed his way back through the brush leading the Ovaro behind him until he emerged near the mouth of the cave and carefully obliterated hoofmarks with a piece of branch until the only ones left were those that went on up the passage. Satisfied, he returned to the cave and found Clover had a small fire lighted up against the back wall of the second opening.

"They outside looking for us?" she asked.

"Near enough. If they follow the passage they'll go past us," he said. "Then they'll hole in someplace for the night and wait for morning."

"What do we do? Go on when it gets dark?" she asked.

"No, we won't be able to make enough time and both Polly's sidewinders and Dandridge's have settled in someplace up here, you can be sure. I don't want us blundering smack into them," he said. "I'll do some night scouting alone so we can be ready to move out, come dawn."

"It's really me they want," Clover said. "They're still afraid I know the things Rosalyn Tremayne knew."

"Well, I've been in it since that morning I saved you from a necktie party. Can't quit now."

Her eyes regarded him gravely, her pert face still clouded with somber feelings. "I don't want to stay here alone. What if a bear lives here? Or a cougar?" she glowered.

"That's what the fire is for. Just keep it going and

stay beside it and you'll be fine until I get back," Fargo told her.

"Safe, maybe, but not fine," she muttered, and he laughed as he went to check the horses and be sure they were well tethered.

"Be back soon as I can," he said, and was about to turn away when she bounded up and flew against him, her mouth reaching up to press hard against his lips. Just as suddenly she pulled away, her face grave. She folded herself beside the fire and didn't look up at him again.

He hurried out of the cave. Outside, he peered at the moon, which had come up to outline the hills in its ghost-white paleness. He moved forward and settled into a long, wolflike lope that let him achieve distance with a minimum of effort and energy. He moved along the creviced passage, a silent, wraithlike figure in the night, and he used his nose and his ears as much as he did his eyes as he climbed the hills. To his left, and not that far away, he heard a horse blow air. Dooley's camp, he grunted. But the others were somewhere in the hills and it was obvious they'd set a plan and so far were holding to it.

In the moon's fitful light he followed the pattern of the hills with his eyes as he halted, dropped to one knee, and rested. A deep gorge held his gaze. It cut across the middle of the hills, the only passage from one side to the other a narrow, slat-wood bridge just wide enough for one rider at a time. He rose and went on until he was close to the gorge and the wood bridge and he surveyed the approaches. There were three that came out close to the bridge and two more a few hundred yards on, and he fixed each approach in his mind as he went on.

When he turned and began to retrace steps down the hills, the dawn was fast approaching. But he'd enough time to reach the cave and he'd let himself sleep a few hours into the morning. Dooley and the others would be scouring the woods with the first light. It was best to make a move later in the morning when they'd tired themselves out some.

Fargo hurried downward in the long, loping gait until he reached the brush-covered mouth of the cave. He saw the first streaks of dawn edging across the sky as he slipped through the brush and into the cave. He hurried around the bend and saw the fire was almost out, but there was no one beside it. "Clover?" he called out, instant apprehension seizing hold of him and his hand was on the butt of the big Colt at his hip as he turned to the horses. But there was only one horse, the Ovaro, and he was at it in a half-dozen long strides as he spotted the torn piece of notepaper stuck under the edge of the saddle.

He pulled it free, brought it to the fire, and sank down on one knee to get enough light to read the penciled words.

> It's really me they want. I know it. I won't let them kill you just to get me. You've done too much for me for that. It's time I returned the favor.

"Damn her stubborn hide," he swore aloud as he crumpled the note in his hand and tossed it into the remains of the fire. He pulled himself onto the Ovaro and sent the horse out of the cave into the pink-gray light of the new day that was already embracing the hills. He frowned down at the ground and picked up the tracks of her horse. She had cut across the slope, riding hard, and had swung up along a rain-washed gulley that formed a wide swath. He cursed and knew his only hope was that she had put enough distance on before Dooley and his posse had begun to ride. He was beginning to think that perhaps she'd pulled it off when he saw the horsemen, strung out in pairs, racing along the top of a rocky rise. He swung his gaze forward and saw Clover with the nearest of Dooley's men closing in on her.

"Shit," he murmured, and swung a glance in a fast circle across the rest of the hills. He spied the second set of riders appear from far to the left and, swinging his gaze again, the third set from the right. He brought his eyes back to Clover as the first two riders with Dooley right behind closed in on her. She tried to swerve as she heard the whistle of a lariat spinning through the air, but she was too late and the lasso fell around her shoulders. The men pulled the lasso closed and yanked back, but Clover held on to her saddle horn with both hands and avoided being yanked from the horse. Slowed to an abrupt halt, the horse bucked and stopped, and Fargo saw the two men pull Clover to them. Dooley came up to her. They threw another rope around her and brought her along between the two riders as the others fell in behind, Dooley half-hidden behind a big, burly man.

Fargo halted at the edge of a slab of granite and saw Dandridge and his band drawing closer. He glanced the other way and saw Polly leading her posse up. He grimaced but drew the big Sharps from its saddle holster. It wouldn't set Clover free, but it'd cut down the odds a little and help him get rid of some of the frustration that had seized him. He raised the rifle, took aim, and fired, two quick shots that resounded from the rocks. One of Dooley's men flew from his horse as he clapped both hands to his head. The one next to him fell forward across his horse's neck and hung there for a moment before sliding slowly and lifelessly to the ground.

Fargo saw Dooley leap for cover, dropping from his horse on the far side, and the others wheeled and scattered, but the two holding Clover held on to her as they sent their horses darting for cover behind the rocks. "Down there. Get him," he heard Dooley shout, and three of his men started to come forward.

Fargo fired again and they took cover at once but Dandridge and his men were drawing uncomfortably close. Polly, too, he saw, and he turned the Ovaro and sent the horse streaking across the slope. He turned downhill, took a narrow path upward, and held on it into the higher rises. He circled, came back on a high ledge, and moved the Ovaro out boldly, gazing down at where Polly and Dandridge had brought their men together with Ed Dooley's band.

He saw one of the men look up and spot him and all of them followed his shout. Fargo smiled grimly. They turned and, with Clover held in front of Dooley, began to move slowly through the hills. He rode with them on the high land, making no effort to hide. It was what they expected, and he'd give them what they expected for the moment. They rode unhurriedly and paused at midday to eat. Fargo did the same as he stayed in view of them. When they moved on, he moved along above them and saw they were nearing the deep gorge through the hills. They turned as they drew closer and rode parallel to the cut until dusk began to slide over the land.

Fargo watched Dooley and his men draw to a halt while Polly went on in one direction and Dandridge in the other. Fargo halted, let himself fade out of their sight among the high rocks, and swung from his horse. He stretched and sat down against a tall rock as night descended. He waited until the moon rose before he moved forward to peer down at the campsite below. Clover, wrists and ankles bound, lay on the ground while Dooley and his men had bedded down to one side of the site, and again Fargo smiled. They had staked out the bait and waited for him to take it. He was certain that Dandridge's men were hidden to one side, waiting for him to come that way, and Polly's on the other. It was transparent, but they counted on his going to save Clover one more time.

Their thinking was right in that, Fargo sniffed silently, only he wouldn't do it their way and just take the bait they offered. He started downhill, left the Ovaro a little more than halfway down, and changed directions on foot. On steps silent as a bobcat's tread, he moved to the right as he continued downward, and Polly's camp came into sight pretty much where he'd expected to find it, behind a cluster of oaks but close enough for her sentries to watch any approach to Clover. The first man appeared directly below him, sitting with his back against a tree and facing Dooley's campsite. Fargo's eyes swept the darkness and picked out two more men, each facing the approaches to Dooley's site, and he began to creep downward toward the first.

He moved on careful, silent steps, but he knew these were no mountain men with the hearing of a white-tailed doe and no woodsmen with the inner acuity of the red-tailed hawk. These were only hired guns—and not very good ones at that—and he crept upon the first one without trouble and brought the butt of the big Colt down on the man's head and the figure fell over on his side. The second was just as easy, but the third decided to rise, turn, and stretch just as Fargo was almost at him. An expression of surprise and then alarm leapt into the man's face as Fargo swung a long, looping right that hit on the point of the man's jaw. As the man staggered backward, Fargo leapt and smashed the barrel of the Colt across his head. The man crumpled at his feet and lay still. Fargo stepped over him with disdain and hurried down the few remaining yards to where three more men lay asleep and, at one side, Polly slept inside a blanket.

He stepped around to the back side of the small area and came up on the woman, knelt on one knee, and pressed a hand over her face. Her eyes snapped open instantly and she saw the barrel of the Colt at her temple. "You even breath hard and my finger will press this trigger," he whispered. "I'm very nervous." The madam's eyes narrowed in anger and disbelief, but she knew the threat was no exercise in emptiness. She rose with him and he saw she was dressed under the blanket except for her shirt, which she scooped up from the ground. He nodded and kept the gun pressed to her temple as he took her into the trees and moved uphill with her. She pulled her shirt on as they walked, and when he was far enough from the camp, he lowered the Colt.

"You won't get away with it, you know," she snapped. "Even if you get her back, you won't get away."

"One thing at a time," Fargo said almost cheerfully, and she flung daggers of fury at him with her eyes. He halted beside the Ovaro and led the way back toward Dooley's campsite. With a length of lariat, he tied Polly to a tree and settled himself on the ground. "I'll make it very simple for you, honey. I still owe you for having that goddamn giant try to kill me. It'll be light in a few hours. They kill Clover and I kill you. They let her go and I let you go. Simple. I'll even let you explain it to them."

"You still won't get away. There are two many of us," the madam said.

"I've got plans." Fargo smiled, put his head back, and closed his eyes. He half-slept, heard Polly trying to pull free, and continued to doze.

The new sun woke him as it came over the tops of the hills and he rose and saw that Polly had slumped down to the ground. She opened her eyes as he untied her and pushed to her feet. He led her by the elbow as he went another dozen yards closer to the campsite below. He halted and saw Dooley come into sight and yank Clover to her feet.

"Maybe he ain't comin' for you, doll," he heard Dooley snarl at Clover.

"He's coming for her," Fargo called out, and Dooley spun, yanking at his six-gun as he peered up at the hill. Fargo saw the man frown up at him and the others gather behind him.

163

"Dammit, Polly, that you?" Dooley called.

"It's me," the woman snapped, and Fargo waited until he heard the rustle of shrub and Dandridge came into the camp with his men to stare up at the hillside along with Dooley.

"You want to explain it, honey?" Fargo said to Polly, and she threw him a glare of pure hate.

"Let the little bitch go for now," the madam called down.

"What do you mean let her go?" Dooley frowned.

"He'll kill me if you don't," Polly said, and Fargo watched Dooley and Dandridge exchange hurried whispers.

"She stays here," Dooley said when their exchange ended. "You want her, you come down here. Maybe we can talk this out."

Fargo laughed, a bitter sound, and drew his six-gun and placed the barrel against Polly's temple. "Let Clover go or she's dead," he called down.

"He's not the bluffing kind," Polly shouted. "Let her go for now, dammit."

"No dice," Dandridge said.

"What's the matter with you? He's going to kill me," Polly shouted, rage and disbelief in her voice.

"We don't give a shit," Dooley shouted back. "We got the girl and we're going to close her mouth for good."

"Real nice partners you have there, Polly," Fargo commented.

"You bastards. You stinking sons of bitches," the madam screamed down at the two men.

"Tough," Dandridge returned. "You don't mean shit to us. She does."

Fargo kept the gun at Polly's head as he cursed

silently. It was a turn he hadn't expected. Their attitude gave him no cards to play with, no bargaining leverage. He swore again inwardly and took the gun from Polly's temple. "Maybe you're right. Maybe we can talk this out," he said, choosing his words carefully. They wanted him dead, too. He'd toss them a few crumbs and let them think that maybe they could have everything they wanted. "If I let her go, you promise we can talk? No tricks?" he asked.

"You've our word on that, Fargo," Dooley said after a quick exchange of glances with Dandridge, and Fargo held a bitter snort inside himself.

"I'll have to think some more on it," he said, and started to back up the hill, pulling Polly along with him. He disappeared into the trees and saw Polly was frowning at him.

"This isn't you," she murmured, watching him closely.

"One for you," Fargo grunted. "They're real loyal, those partners of yours."

Her eyes flashed fury instantly. "Those rotten bastards. We had an agreement. Those no good, double-crossing pricks," she rasped.

"You want to stay alive?" he asked harshly, and the woman nodded. "Then you do exactly what I say. You stay here. Give me fifteen minutes and start walking down the hill to Dooley. They'll be watching you come down to them, and so will I. You make one wrong move and I'll put a bullet right through your head. You can count on it," he told her.

"I just walk down the hill to them?" she echoed.

"That's all," Fargo said. "But this gun's going to

be right on you." He saw her thoughts whirling. "You don't carry a shitful of weight to those two. You know that now."

"Yes, goddamn their stinkin' souls. I know that now," she said.

"Make your mind up. A chance to walk away alive or be loyal to those two weasels down there."

"I'll walk," the woman bit out, and he nodded, took the Ovaro, and started to go deeper into the trees.

"Fifteen minutes," he called back, and vanished into the thick foliage. He swung onto his horse and rode downhill in a wide circle until he had reached the bottom, where he turned and started to move up to the back edge of the campsite. He dismounted when he got near and went on foot, pulling the horse behind him. He heard the murmur of voices as he neared the campsite from the rear. He came as close as he dared with the horse and then went the rest of the way alone. He halted at the thick shrubs at the back edge of the campsite and peered forward, the Colt in his hand. Dooley and Dandridge were together, peering up at the hill, their hired hands spread out along the sides. He spotted Clover, standing with her wrists bound, alone a few yards from Dooley. He felt tiny drops of perspiration form on his forehead and swore silently.

It could work if the madam played it straight. He counted on the icy rage inside her to keep her in line. They had been willing to sacrifice her without a second thought. She wanted to pay them back for that. Maybe after a day or two she'd simmer down, but now she was feeling betrayed and double-crossed. He counted on her fury to make her play it his way.

But he sweated. He always hated counting on some-one like Polly, but he had no choice. He crouched, waited, and saw her emerge from the trees.

She started down the hillside and he saw Dooley and Dandridge watching her. She was nearly at the bottom when Dooley called out. "Where is he?" the man asked.

"He said he'd be along," Polly answered.

Fargo rose to his feet, but stayed crouched low. Dooley and Dandridge were completely concentrat-ing on watching Polly approach. It was now or never, Fargo realized.

"Don't move, either of you," he said from the bushes. "Move a finger and you're both dead men." He saw Dooley and Dandridge freeze in place and Dandridge start to turn his head. "I said, don't move," Fargo snapped, and the man froze in posi-tion. He'd been going to call to Clover but he didn't need to, he saw, as she'd begun to run toward him. His eyes swept the hired guns standing along the sides, uncertain, watching, waiting for an order. "Tell them not to do the wrong thing or you're both dead," Fargo said to Dooley, and saw the man swallow hard.

"Stay there, don't move," Dooley told the oth-ers, and Fargo watched them stay in place.

"Over here," he called to Clover as she moved to him. He had the double-bladed throwing knife out of its calf holster when she broke through the brush. He severed her wrist bonds with one thrust and gestured to the Ovaro. As she swung onto the horse, he heard Dooley snarl at Polly.

"You bitch," the man rasped. "You helped him set us up."

"I saved my life, which is more than you bastards were going to do," Polly shouted back, and as Fargo leapt onto the Ovaro, he saw Dooley yank his six-gun and fire, the shot slamming into the madam's midsection.

"Damn," Fargo said, and sent the Ovaro into a gallop that broke through the brush.

He saw Dooley whirl and shout, "Get them, goddammit."

Fargo reined up just enough to level the big Colt. He fired over the top of the brush and Ed Dooley's head exploded in a shower of red spray and Dandridge ducked away. Fargo sent the Ovaro racing forward again and heard the others gathering themselves, leaping onto their horses. But he had almost a full minute's start and he knew exactly where he was going. He sent the Ovaro racing uphill as Clover clung to him.

"You are getting to be a real pain in the ass, you know that?" he growled at her.

"It was the right thing to do," she muttered.

"It was the stupid thing to do."

"You could've gone your way," she said.

"I could've done that that first morning," he returned, and she made a face. "Besides, they'd have come after me," he added. He gave a bitter snort as he heard the thunder of hoofbeats in pursuit.

Dandridge was still there. They still had a leader to pay them off, he grunted as he veered the pinto through a narrow passage. The gorge came into view, deeper than it had seemed at night, the wood-slat bridge even narrower. He raced for it as the land leveled off and slowed the horse when he neared the closest end of the bridge. He wanted them to think they were closing in on him and he waited until he saw the riders come into sight, Dandridge in the lead.

Fargo put the Ovaro into a gallop and reached the bridge, swerved, and raced across it. On the other side he disappeared into the trees, reined to a sharp halt, and yanked the big Sharps from its saddle case as he leapt from the saddle.

He dropped to one knee, took aim, and waited as Dandridge led the charge across the bridge, the others single-file behind him. He drew a careful bead on the man, waiting till he was almost at the other end of the span, and he fired. The shot slammed into Dandridge and he flew from his horse, hit the rope side of the bridge, and jackknifed into the gorge. He was only a falling object at the periphery of Fargo's vision as he sent another bullet into the second rider, two more into the third and fourth. Their horses slowed and the others following jammed into them. Fargo drew the Colt and began to fire with speed and accuracy. He saw at least four figures plunge over the side of the bridge and into the gorge. Another man screamed in pain as a shot caught him in the leg. He fell, rolled, and plunged over the edge of the bridge, his screams echoing all the way to the bottom.

Others had leapt from their horses and were racing from the bridge as a few more managed to back their mounts off the narrow path.

Fargo rose, drew a deep sigh, slowly reloaded, and saw Clover come toward him. "It's over now," he said. "The rest are just hired hands. They'll be happy to get the hell away with their lives and whatever advance money they were paid." Clover came to rest against him, her arms around his waist, and he watched the riderless horses make their way from the narrow bridge. "Time to go," he said, and she nodded and climbed onto the Ovaro with him.

"We'll take our time going back," she murmured.

"Just what I planned to do," Fargo said.

She gave a satisfied little sound and clung to him. "Too bad you couldn't have collected that reward Abbot Tremayne offered for his brother's killer," she said. "You could've been rolling in clover."

"I figure I'll be doing that anyway." He grinned.

"Yes, oh, yes, you will," she agreed happily.

LOOKING FORWARD!
The following is the opening
section from the next novel in the exciting
Trailsman series from Signet:

The Trailsman #73
Santa Fe Slaughter

July, 1861. In remote Santa Fe,
the mountain-rimmed capital of the
Territory of New Mexico, where intrigue
and suspicion are rampant . . .

Silent rage flowed across the table in mounting heated waves that Skye Fargo could almost feel, but he stayed calm as he stretched his long legs and settled back in his ornately carved wooden chair. Then he glared straight back at Cyrus Ashbrook.

"I know you've got plenty of problems, Mr. Ashbrook," Fargo said while toying with a toothpick, "but I didn't suspect that one of them was a hearing problem. Watch and listen real close here. My answer is no. N-O. Absolutely no. Definitely not. You've made it clear that taking the job means doing things your way. And when I work, I do things my way." Fargo paused to pick his teeth before concluding. "Do you understand me this time?"

All of Ashbrook's chins—at least three, although in the dim interior of a Santa Fe cantina, it was hard to get an exact count—started to quiver as his wispy white muttonchops bristled. The fleshy man had already drunk too much to be very civil. His beady bloodshot eyes glowed as he surveyed his three associates for reinforcement before returning to meet Fargo's icy visage.

But it was Chester Eakins, the gaunt man on Ashbrook's right, who pursued the appeal. He talked in a more reasonable and less imperious tone, re-phrasing what Ashbrook had already said. "Mr. Fargo, it's like this. You know we're all merchants here in Santa Fe. We've got to have goods to sell, goods that come in by wagon train. Somebody's hitting our wagon trains on the way in, and sometimes even on the way out, even when all they've got aboard is that rough Mexican wool. It doesn't happen on every trip, but it happens often enough to where we can't hire crews."

"No, that's not quite right," interjected Josiah Watson, the dapper little man at the far right. "You can always hire crews—drifters, no-accounts, riff-raff. Any of the good wagon men, though, can find all the work they want with other outfits. They're going around mean-mouthing us, saying that no-body in their right minds would work for us."

Fargo took in the cantina with his lake-blue eyes. This early in the evening, and with no recent wagon train arrivals or similar inducements to free spending, they were the only patrons. He spied the waitress emerging from the dark kitchen entrance, on her way to their table, before answering. "Likely the wagon men are right," he replied. "Nobody in his right mind would work for you. As best I know, I'm still in my right mind."

The waitress arrived at their massive round table and began picking up the remains of their dinner, huge tortillas rolled around melted goat cheese, chopped beef, and refried beans, smothered in green chili hot enough to burn a new asshole into a man, washed down with cold beer. It was food Fargo loved, and even the fact that he'd been eating with a bunch of nincompoop storekeepers didn't diminish that pleasure.

For one thing, they were paying for the meal. They'd made such a production out of inviting Fargo to "discuss important, confidential business" that he'd even smoothed back his shoulder-length black hair. He has even considered getting his full beard trimmed before recalling that not one of the six barber chairs in Santa Fe was built for comfortable sitting by any man much over six feet tall.

Fargo gazed appreciatively at the waitress as she removed his plate, especially enjoying the view when she bent to reach for an errant fork and revealed the substantial curvature that her low-cut blouse had advertised.

Her appearance reminded Fargo why he liked Santa Fe so much. In most other western towns, the womenfolk tended to be pale, pinch-faced schoolmarms determined to drain every ounce of pleasure out of life. As soon as they arrived, they agitated against saloons and gambling halls. They set up Sunday schools. They swooned when they heard someone say "leg." They wore at least four layers of clothes and felt violated if a man saw an ankle or elbow.

But the earthy women of New Mexico Territory weren't new arrivals bent on civilizing the heathens. They liked a good time just as much as the men did. They danced all night at fandangos in their gaudy scooped blouses and shamefully short skirts. They drank openly, right next to the men, while they laughed and flirted. They even smoked in public, not cigars like the men, but something they called "cigarillos"—a pinch or two of tobacco rolled up in a cornhusk or leaf of paper torn out of an old Bible. The *señoritas* of Santa Fe never worried too much about what Queen Victoria might say, so they just enjoyed each day to the fullest.

In the cool of this evening in early July, with unspent coins jingling in his pocket, Fargo couldn't think of a better place to spend a few weeks. And he could think of some worse ways to pass time, such as scouring the desert along both sides of six hundred miles of Santa Fe Trail on a wild-goose chase, which was what these men had in mind.

Chester Eakins sported an immense beaklike nose that must have sniffed Fargo's thoughts. As soon as the waitress was out of earshot, he warily eyed everyone at the table and began speaking in a low and conspiratorial tone.

"Mr. Fargo, it's like this. Your search wouldn't be that difficult, because we know who's robbing our wagon trains. All you have to do is catch them. You're the Trailsman, the one can track down anybody, so it should be easy once we tell you who's behind all this."

"And who might that be?" Fargo asked, settling into comfort with a good meal inside him and good beer in front of him. These men were stupid and disgusting, but not quite so disgusting that he felt any desire to stir.

Eakins glanced around again before leaning over to Fargo. "It's Russell, Majors, and Waddell. They're already the biggest freighting company in America, and they're fixing to get bigger. They're hitting our trains so they can drive all us little guys out of business. Then they'll have a monopoly on the Santa Fe trade."

Fargo slid his chair even farther back and began laughing so hard that he came close to falling out of his seat. "Jesus H. Christ," he exclaimed, catching his breath, "they're so big that you're not even a pimple on their ass."

Ashbrook leaned forward, knocking over his beer bottle. The amber liquid dripped back over his lap as he scowled at Fargo. "All right, Mr. Fargo, I can see that you don't believe what must be the truth. Who else could be hitting our wagon trains?"

"Who else?" Fargo asked, sitting up straight after his attack of laughter. "From here to Missouri, there's Indians: Comanche, Kiowa, Jicarilla Apache, Pawnee, Cheyenne, Osage, Kansas. They've all been known to bother wagons. Then there are the Comancheros, who don't do much else besides raid, rape, and plunder."

Ashbrook's grimace hadn't worked itself into a growl yet, so Fargo continued. "You've got a lot of Mexican folks around here who are still mad about the way things turned out back in 1846, and they figure it's their patriotic duty to pester gringos. Besides that, New Mexico Territory attracts hard cases and outlaws the way shit draws flies. I see pictures of your leading citizens hanging on the wall every time I go into a post office."

Before Ashbrook could interrupt, Fargo swigged the rest of his beer and concluded. "I don't take jobs unless I'm sure I can do them, and I don't see any way to do yours the way you want it done."

"Are you sure?" Ashbrook fumed as his three associates pretended to ignore the sloppy way the man grabbed Eakins' beer and got most of it on his linen shirt. "Could it be, Mr. Fargo, that you're a coward, that you're afraid to take a job that's right along your line?"